PUFFIN BOOKS

Scarper Jack

& THE BLOODSTAINED ROOM

Violent Struggle. Bloody Murder.
Doors and Windows Locked and Bolted.
No Way In or Out. Mystery.
Impossible Crime. Bloody Murder.
MURDER. NUNWELL STREET!

Jack dropped the newspaper and rushed round the end of the houses and along the back alleyway to the shared privy, reaching it just in time before he was violently sick.

On his knees, shaking with nausea and shock, he confronted the truth. There had indeed been a killing.

And he knew where the murderer lived.

Christopher Russell was a postman when he had his first radio play broadcast in 1975, having given up a job in the civil service to do shift work and have more daytime hours for writing. Since 1980, he has been a full-time scriptwriter and has worked on numerous television and radio programmes. Christopher lives with his wife on the Isle of Wight.

Books by Christopher Russell

BRIND AND THE DOGS OF WAR

PLAGUE SORCERER

SCARPER JACK AND THE BLOODSTAINED ROOM

SMUGGLERS

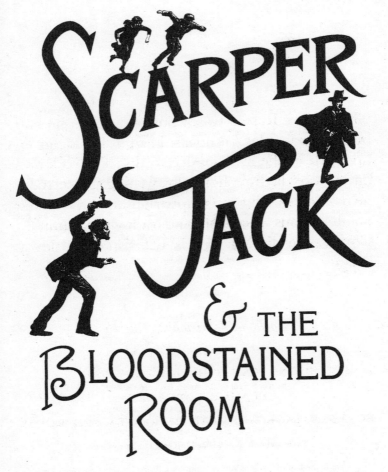

SCARPER JACK

& THE BLOODSTAINED ROOM

BY
CHRISTOPHER RUSSELL

PUFFIN

PUFFIN BOOKS

Published by the Penguin Group
Penguin Books Ltd, 80 Strand, London WC2R ORL, England
Penguin Group (USA) Inc., 375 Hudson Street, New York, New York 10014, USA
Penguin Group (Canada), 90 Eglinton Avenue East, Suite 700, Toronto, Ontario, Canada M4P 2Y3
(a division of Pearson Penguin Canada Inc.)
Penguin Ireland, 25 St Stephen's Green, Dublin 2, Ireland (a division of Penguin Books Ltd)
Penguin Group (Australia), 250 Camberwell Road, Camberwell, Victoria 3124, Australia
(a division of Pearson Australia Group Pty Ltd)
Penguin Books India Pvt Ltd, 11 Community Centre, Panchsheel Park, New Delhi – 110 017, India
Penguin Group (NZ), 67 Apollo Drive, Rosedale, North Shore 0632, New Zealand
(a division of Pearson New Zealand Ltd)
Penguin Books (South Africa) (Pty) Ltd, 24 Sturdee Avenue, Rosebank,
Johannesburg 2196, South Africa

Penguin Books Ltd, Registered Offices: 80 Strand, London WC2R ORL, England

puffinbooks.com

First published 2008
1

Copyright © Christopher Russell, 2008
All rights reserved

The moral right of the author has been asserted

Set in Baskerville MT
Typeset by Palimpsest Book Production Limited, Grangemouth, Stirlingshire

Made and printed in England by Clays Ltd, St Ives plc

British Library Cataloguing in Publication Data
A CIP catalogue record for this book is available from the British Library

ISBN: 978-0-141-32258-2

This book is dedicated to Londoner Ben

Contents

I

Voices in the Chimney

'Hello, son.'

The man on the doorstep smiled. Easy, confident, sure of his welcome. The boy just stared at him. Shocked.

'Who is it, Jack?' wheezed a voice from the parlour across the narrow hallway.

'My father,' said the boy, still staring. Then he turned from the door, leaving the man he hadn't seen for three years to follow if he chose.

Arthur Jevons looked up from his chair. The effort of speaking tightened his chest.

'And what would he be wanting?' he asked, regarding the man but addressing the boy.

Jack guessed the answer would be to no one's advantage except his father's.

'Tony Tolchard,' announced the new arrival, with the merest nod of acknowledgement at Jevons. 'Come to reclaim his son.'

He turned to Jack and sounded hurt; a loving parent spurned by his thoughtless child.

'I've just looked for you at Sparshott's,' he said. 'Why did you leave him? Why didn't you tell me?'

'I didn't know where you were,' Jack managed to reply.

He'd got over the shock now. His cheeks were burning. He'd known he'd been sold to his first employer, Sparshott. Even at the age of eight, he'd noticed the money changing hands.

'Sparshott's the cruellest villain in the business,' growled Jevons.

'He says you stole my son from him,' said Tony, turning a righteous glare in his direction.

'Rescued him,' said Jevons firmly despite his wheezing. 'Rescued him.'

'That's noble,' sneered Tony. 'One sweep from another.'

'Sparshott puts his boys up chimneys.' A coughing spasm interrupted Jevons. Eventually, he recovered. 'It's illegal. Perhaps you didn't know what would happen to your son. Or care?'

'No one cares more for Jack than I do,' snapped Tony. Then he shrugged. 'Life was difficult when we first came to London. After our loss.' He looked with sad appeal at the woman he assumed was Jevons' wife, sitting on the other side of the small fire with her collection of silent children. 'Jack will have told you, ma'am, of the death of his mother and sister.' He lowered his eyes. 'I'm man enough, I hope, to admit that in my grief I made mistakes. If Sparshott was a hard master then I'm sorry for it.'

He shrugged again, the subject dismissed, as if selling his eight-year-old child had been nothing to be ashamed of. Jack had been a slave to Sparshott for three years, living in fear, misery and squalor before Mr Jevons had saved him. Now his father was here, acting hurt. Jack could scarcely believe it. His father merely smiled at him and continued briskly.

'But that's all in the past. I have a steady job now and decent lodgings. It's time for me to be a proper father once again. To make amends. So, Jack, fetch your coat if you have one: you're coming home with me.'

'Make amends?' asked Jevons. 'Or take his wages? Now he's old enough to earn more. Is that it?'

Tony snorted with contempt. 'No. But if it was, I'd find him a better job than this.'

Jack didn't move.

Did he have a duty to this father who had sold him to be put up chimneys and left him to his fate for three long years before he was rescued? Surely, his greater duty was to Arthur Jevons, who had been kind and was now ill. Jack had been well fed and cared for by the Jevons family and was now the strong lad needed here. He looked to his master for guidance. For help.

'Is that what you desire, Jack?' The sweep's tone, like his watery eyes, was as mild as usual.

'What he desires,' cut in Tony, 'or you persuade him to desire at this moment, is of no matter. I'm his father. His legal guardian.' He didn't turn to Jack as he spoke again, firmly. 'Fetch your coat.'

Jack didn't move, just continued to look helplessly at his master. Eventually, Jevons blinked and gave the slightest of nods. Jack turned towards his father, then stopped and looked back at Jevons.

'I shall be back at eight in the morning,' he promised. 'To help you in Calborn Gardens.'

He glanced defiantly at his father, his face flushed, but received only a bland smile in return. He hurried out.

As they walked down the street, Tony put a companionable arm round Jack's stiff shoulders.

'We shall have good times together,' he said. 'Were you ever in a public house?'

Jack shook his head.

His father tutted. 'But you're almost a man. You do know what tomorrow is?'

Jack nodded. 'My birthday,' he said dully.

'Your twelfth birthday.' The correction was cheerily emphatic. 'And we shall celebrate in proper style. Father and son.'

His father strode on, his arm still round Jack's

shoulder; and the shabby warmth of the Jevons household faded behind them.

As promised, Jack was back at the sweep's yard next morning, slipping away from his new home before his father was awake. Neither he nor Mr Jevons spoke of the change in Jack's circumstances as they rode away to Calborn Gardens on the sweep's horse-drawn cart.

Number twelve Calborn Gardens was a fine terraced house, as tall and elegant as its owner, or at least, its owner's wife, Mrs Shorey.

She was a regular customer of Jevons the sweep and trusted him. She didn't hover in the background while he spread his dust sheets and assembled his connecting rods and brushes, but was happy to leave him to get on with it, even when he was working in the upstairs rooms as he was today.

The Shoreys had a son called Rupert, whom both parents referred to in their amiably remote way as Rupe – a shortening that he tolerated rather than enjoyed.

Rupert was an only child and disliked school. He was indulged in this by his mother, who wanted him to be happy. So Rupert had been excused the terrors of boarding school at the age of seven and allowed to attend day school instead. He was excused the terrors of day school by regular if vague illnesses which usually coincided with boxing lessons and gymnastics in the school yard. His father occasionally muttered in a disapproving way but didn't interfere.

Rupert was at home now, in his bedroom, which was on the first floor, close to the guest room where the chimney sweep and his boy were working. He was reading a book he'd taken from his father's library downstairs. Mr Shorey was a solicitor and most of his books were boring to Rupert if not actually unreadable, but there was a history shelf on which he could always find something of interest. He liked reading about the past. The past never seemed to involve school.

The bedroom door was open, although it should have been closed to keep out the dust, and Rupert couldn't help looking out. He rather envied the sweep's boy: his life was almost certainly free of mathematics tests and fourth-form bullies.

'Are you having difficulties, Mr Jevons?'

Mrs Shorey was in the guest-room doorway. The enquiry was patient and kindly but Jevons was defensive. A brush had jammed in the upper flue.

'No, ma'am. Soon be done.'

His voice was thicker than usual. Jack knew the signs. It wasn't just the soot. Anxiety always made his breathing worse. The job was taking far longer than it should.

'My husband wonders that you don't use one of the new machines.'

'Does he, ma'am?' wheezed Jevons non-committally, without turning from the fireplace where he crouched. Mr Shorey was always wondering about the new machines. Arthur Jevons couldn't afford a new machine. He depended entirely on Jack and now was likely to lose even him.

'Did Elizabeth bring your tea?'

'No, ma'am, thank you kindly.'

'She forgets everything. I shall have it sent up directly.'

Jack heard Mrs Shorey rustle away behind them. He was pleased about the tea. Sweeping was thirsty work and this was the only house where refreshment was offered. But he was worried about his master, who suddenly slumped backwards and sat convulsed, struggling to keep a coughing fit politely silent. Sweat sprang from his grimy contorted face. When at last he was able to speak again, his voice was an unintentional whisper. He nodded at the fireplace and the connecting rod just visible.

'I can't shift it, Jack.'

'I'll do it.'

Jack put a hand briefly on Jevons' shoulder and moved towards the fireplace.

'No, Jack, you mustn't . . .'

The sweep's protest was real but feeble.

'Don't worry.' Jack's reply was also quiet. 'I'll get out in the attic – no one will know. I'll see you downstairs.'

Out on the landing, Rupert was peeping. He watched the sweeping boy's bare feet disappear up the guest-room chimney.

The flue was narrow but Jack was skinny. A little too tall perhaps: he'd outgrown the stunted tinyness of the natural climbing boy that had so pleased Sparshott, his first master. Instead, he now had a strength that enabled him to writhe upwards in the dark, using his toes almost like claws. The brickwork here was rough but at least cool: the fireplace in the guest room wasn't used every day and most of the soot had already been scoured away by the brush now jammed somewhere above him.

Jack found and unscrewed the last connection and lowered the rod down the chimney beneath him. He felt Jevons take it and draw it out of the fireplace below. He had a little more room to move in now, with the rod out of the way, and inched his way upwards again, groping above his head for the brush itself, which would be wedged between inconvenient outcrops of brick. As he did so, he heard two voices, muffled but close. Jack listened and soon realized they came from the house next door.

'So you can help me?'

'Of course. Anything can be done for money.'

'How much?'

'A hundred pounds. Cash.'

There was a brief pause.

'Very well. But it must be done tonight – before midnight at the latest.'

'But after dark, I hope? I'm not invisible.'

'Of course, but as soon as possible.'

'The address?'

'Nunwell Street.'

'Number?'

Jack slipped slightly and didn't hear the answer clearly. Seventeen? Seventy? Or twenty? Or seven D?

He held his breath but the quiet conversation continued. No one had heard him, or at least, no one seemed to have associated the small sound of falling soot with the presence of a boy, close behind the chimney wall.

'The money within two days.'

'Yes. How will you do it?'

'What's that to you, as long as he's dead?'

The other voice didn't reply immediately and Jack heard no more as the speakers moved to the far end of the room, muttering.

Jack forced himself to climb upwards. He found the brush and wrenched it free, then climbed higher still before slithering downwards into a short, adjoining flue that brought him out into the fireplace of the Shoreys' attic. What should he do?

The disused attic was empty and stifling. Jack felt the need of fresh air. He opened the window and climbed out, hoisting himself up on to the slates above, climbing to the roof ridge and straddling it, his back leaning against the chimney stack. He usually thought more clearly on a rooftop, though at this moment he was too shocked to think at all. He'd occasionally overheard voices before, from within a chimney. Usually children playing in nurseries. Never murder being planned. He rehearsed the conversation in his head. Hoping to find some other, innocent meaning in the words so that he could laugh at himself for being stupid. But it didn't work. There was no alternative meaning; no matter how distorted the voices had been through the chimney. Someone was being paid to kill someone else. Tonight.

Rupert had been intrigued by the sweeping boy's disappearance. There was a fire escape at the end of the corridor near his bedroom and the guest room, and he crept along to it now, pushed open the fire-escape door and emerged on to the small, square metal landing outside. Had the boy popped out of the chimney pot after his brush? Was that possible? Rupert didn't think so. But he couldn't see the chimney stack from the fire escape, so he trotted quietly down the iron steps into the back garden and squinted up from there.

Jack heard the footsteps on the fire escape, then saw the Shoreys' son in the garden far below, staring up at him. Why was he doing that? Jack felt vulnerable; and unaccountably guilty. He quickly clambered out of sight down the hidden slope of the roof.

At the same time, in another part of London, a ceremony was taking place. A large, well-dressed man was cutting a ribbon. His name was Henry Featherstone.

'I declare the Prince's Bridge open,' he boomed, oblivious to the chilly wind across the water.

The new steel bridge stretched away before him across the River Thames. Soon it would carry a railway, another link in the ever-growing web of lines that radiated from the capital. Railways were the big thing now. They were expensive to build and the companies that built them needed people like Henry Featherstone to lend them money, so they could buy the steel for the tracks and pay the engineers and workmen who laid them. But there was a big profit in railways because they provided cheap, fast travel. Far faster than horse-drawn carts and carriages. Thousands of ordinary people were eager to buy tickets and ride on the new trains. So investors like Henry Featherstone nearly always got their money back and a fat profit as well. Nearly always.

Featherstone smiled to himself. *I've become like royalty*, he thought, *cutting ribbons, making speeches*. Indeed, he *was* royalty of a kind. The new kind. Businessmen who led the nation's progress. And he liked making speeches; not because he liked the sound of his own voice but because he thought that voice was important. One particular newspaper had called him 'The Voice of the Age' and he was inclined to agree.

'Money,' he now declared, 'and men who are prepared to invest it, are changing the world. Harnessing steam and gas and coal and steel to ever greater purpose. Building stronger bridges, faster railways, bigger factories, deeper mines, all to the ultimate benefit of not just our fellow countrymen but the whole world. Industry and commerce will bind the nations together more closely than any treaty. Money. Progress. Peace.'

The journalists wrote eagerly in their notebooks. The small invited crowd applauded, including a number of Featherstone's business friends. Mostly they didn't resent their extrovert, self-appointed leader. They were in his shadow but accepted that he was a larger-than-life man with the power to inspire. And those he inspired were more likely to invest money: in their ventures as well as his own.

'Mr Featherstone,' said a journalist with a

knowing smile, 'you refer to the whole world. Does that mean your next venture will be beyond these shores?'

Featherstone nodded and returned the smile.

'It does indeed.'

'India?'

Featherstone shook his head.

'Africa?'

Featherstone chuckled teasingly. 'I leave you to speculate, gentlemen. By tomorrow, everything will be in place. Suffice to say it will be my boldest venture yet.'

'Will it be solid?'

Heads turned at the voice. A woman's.

'Or another of your bubbles?'

The woman was trembling, her voice taut. She addressed those around her with bitter scorn.

'You are all fools, hanging on his every word. He can afford to lose. Others can't.' She turned to address Featherstone again.

'Others are drawn in and left penniless. You promised my husband silver from a mine in Cornwall. There is nothing in it, not even tin.'

She began to push her way towards him, her voice and anger rising.

'You boast of benefits for all. Tell me then, where's the benefit in being widowed!'

'Gently, ma'am.' A young man had stepped in front of her, polite but firm.

'I will not be gentle! It's my husband who is dead. My husband who lost our money and with it all his hope and pride! My husband who has hanged himself in shame!'

Fists clenched, she made to fight her way past the young man, then began to sob. The journalists scribbled in their notebooks more eagerly than ever.

'I am sorry, ma'am.' Henry Featherstone's voice was strong but kind. Genuine in its concern. 'There is always risk. I am not King Midas turning everything to gold. Or even silver.'

He did not add that when he'd said his next venture would be his boldest yet, he might have said his wildest. He was risking his entire fortune on three thousand miles of railway line, to run unbroken from Mexico to the tip of South America. As a young man, Henry Featherstone had invested his first pound and made ten. It had been the same ever since: winning, losing. The scale was different, but the thrill never changed. He was currently one of the richest men in England. Next year he might be the poorest. He didn't care.

'Come to my office this evening, ma'am,' he offered, not entirely unaware that the journalists were still writing. 'And I shall find some way to help –'

'Don't insult me with your charity!' screamed the woman.

She flailed at the young man, who still stood in front of her, striking him across the face. She'd recognized him as the great man's son and took a small consolation from the blow. Then she broke away through the crowd and ran off.

Richard Featherstone put his hand to his stinging cheek. Concerned friends of his father clustered round. Avid journalists elbowed in front of them.

'Did you know the woman, sir?'

'No. But she was wrong to spurn my father. His offer was well meant. He's no trickster, as you know. And he cannot be held responsible for the irresponsibility of others. Only gamble what you can afford to lose: print *that* as a warning to all who are tempted to invest.'

'And this great new venture?' asked another journalist slyly. 'Will you give us a hint?'

'I know nothing,' said Richard. 'I never do. Business is my father's domain. Mine is art. You know that too. It would make a pleasant change for the press to gather in such numbers for the unveiling of a marvel of modern painting rather than only marvels of modern engineering. If you'll excuse me.'

And he eased his way towards his father.

In Calborn Gardens, Jack had made a decision: he would not tell Mr Jevons what he had heard.

He feared to worry him. Worry brought on the cough so badly.

Looking down from the roof, he could see the Shoreys' son still in the back garden. Ducking low, so the inquisitive boy wouldn't see him, Jack crept across the rooftops then climbed down a drainpipe at the other end of the row of houses. It wouldn't be the first time he'd removed himself entirely after an illicit chimney climb to help his master.

It wasn't until Jack finally found a policeman that he realized he was still clutching the brush on its short pole. He was also covered in soot.

'Scuse me, sir.'

The policeman turned and looked down at him. The look was suspicious rather than encouraging and it prompted another belated realization. Jack could be getting Mr Jevons into serious trouble: six months in jail for using a climbing boy in a chimney. And not just prison. Hard labour. It would kill him.

'What?' asked the policeman.

Jack was struggling before he started.

'D'you know Nunwell Street?'

'Why?'

'Something's going to happen there tonight.'

'Oh yes?'

'Murder,' said Jack.

The policeman didn't react immediately but then he nodded slightly.

'Oh yes?' he said again. 'And how d'you know that?'

'I don't know what number. I didn't hear – I mean I didn't . . .' Jack knew he was starting to babble. 'Seventeen or seventy or twenty, p'raps seven D. You don't always hear things properly – in a dream.'

He added the last word in desperation and as soon as it was out he knew it was the most stupid of things to say. He'd panicked. The result was inevitable.

'Clear off home and have a wash,' said the policeman and turned away.

At the end of his working day, Jack's father, Tony Tolchard, jingled down the staircase of number seventeen Nunwell Street with an impressive ring of keys in his hand.

He looked in at the front office, where Henry Featherstone was back at a desk piled with folders, ledgers and a litter of loose papers. His son, Richard, was perched by the window. Tony didn't encroach into the room.

'All locked up?' asked Featherstone without turning.

Tony placed the ring of keys on a hook beside the door. 'Yes, sir. Would you like me to fetch anything in for you, sir? For your supper later – a pie, some coffee?'

'Very kind, Tolchard, but no thank you.'

'Right, sir. Goodnight then. Goodnight, Mr Richard.'

'Goodnight, Tolchard.'

As soon as the street door had clicked shut behind his caretaker, Featherstone glanced up at his son.

'Not staying to protect me, are you?'

'Protect you, Pa? From what?'

Featherstone grunted, amused. 'That woman.'

'No,' said Richard, standing up. 'No, I'm not. I have a party to go to.'

His father grunted again, mildly sarcastic this time. 'Another artistic soirée?'

Richard shrugged. 'Just a few friends at the studio – so I'll be at home if you need me.' He moved towards the door. 'But don't let her in, Pa. Seriously. She was half mad. If she had a weapon –'

Featherstone laughed. 'I hope she does come,' he insisted. 'The silver mine was a small but spectacular failure. I should like to help.'

'*Don't* let her in,' repeated Richard.

'Goodnight,' said his father firmly, taking the keys from their hook and following his son to the street door.

Richard heard the key being turned and the two heavy bolts being slid firmly into place even before he'd reached the pavement.

Henry Featherstone returned to his desk. He enjoyed working late, locked in, undistracted. He would be too excited to sleep anyway. Time enough for that when everything was finished. Tomorrow the final visit to the bank. The final signature. All or nothing.

It was almost dark, gas lights illuminating the autumn dusk. Jack hadn't gone home as the policeman had told him. He couldn't. Nunwell Street filled his mind. Eventually he had found it, in the business area of the city, where the streets were lined with banks and offices. Further west the markets and theatres would be filling up with people out to enjoy themselves, but the business area was almost deserted.

Jack walked along the street, surveying the office frontages and their numbers: odds on one side of the road, evens on the other. There was no seven D and no seventy. The evens finished at eighteen, so there was no twenty either. Seventeen then. It must be seventeen.

He retraced his steps. Number seventeen had ground-floor windows behind railings on either side of its front door. The window on one side was heavily curtained, that on the other side was simply dark. The entire building looked blank-faced and devoid of life, like the rest of the street. Jack was seized with sudden doubt. He dithered then walked on. If he met another policeman he would try again. But there was no policeman. At the next junction he halted. Leave or stay? Somehow he couldn't leave, any more than he could bring himself to try knocking at the door of number seventeen. Instead he found his way round behind Nunwell Street.

The back wall of the long terrace of offices rose sheer from a narrow lane, with not even a waterspout near number seventeen, but at the end of the terrace Jack found a drainpipe. He shinned up without difficulty, two storeys to the roof, then made his way quietly across a number of ridges and valleys, counting carefully as he went. He hardly expected to find a murderer lurking but at least from up here he could survey the street from end to end and still make himself heard if a policeman did appear.

In the valley above number seventeen, towards the rear of the building, his toe stubbed against a broken tile. Crouching, he found several others loose. Carefully, he picked one up, to see if there was a hole underneath.

As he did so, he was knocked sprawling on his face by a heavy blow to the head.

2

The Impossible Crime

Jack could hear a noise. He stirred stiffly, feeling cold and wondering where his blanket and pillow had gone. He opened his eyes and could see sky: a few stars above the milky cloud. A clock was chiming. Jack remembered where he was and sat up, putting his hand instinctively to his throbbing head. He felt blood, sticky and congealing.

The clock stopped chiming. At least eight o'clock, perhaps later. Had the thing happened? Had someone actually been killed beneath the roof he'd been lying on? After the chimes there was utter silence. Who or what had hit him? Surely he would have heard someone behind him on the roof. He looked around now as he got gingerly to his feet. The tiled valley was dark and still. Jack felt wobbly. He wanted only to go home. He tripped over the loose tiles but paid them no heed.

As he began shakily to descend the drainpipe, he remembered where home now was.

His father was waiting for him, impatient, clearly ready to go out.

'Where have you been?'

For an instant Jack thought of telling him everything but he didn't get the chance to even start.

'Get yourself cleaned up sharpish,' ordered his father. Then, being met only with a look of confusion, he became angry. 'What's the matter? All that soot getting in your brain? It's your birthday, remember. A *celebration*. Wash yourself and put on a clean shirt. Show a bit of *life*, boy, I'm waiting to spend money on you!'

There was a bucket of water beside the wash bowl. Jack splashed some in and slowly peeled off his shirt. Two minutes later he was being marched through the streets towards the Cap and Cockerel public house.

Tony pushed open the door and thrust Jack inside. The heat and noise battered him and he stepped back, but Tony took his arm again, holding it tight as he wormed his way between the laughing, shouting drinkers. One of the barmaids seemed to know Tony and served him before others already waiting.

'This is him then, is it?' she said, regarding Jack as she drew beer from a tapped barrel.

'This is him. This is my son, Jack. Twelve years old today.'

'A man tomorrow then, eh?'

'And a fine man he'll be,' proclaimed Tony, not just to the barmaid but to the drinkers around him. He wanted a party; to be everybody's friend. Jack was his excuse. He dropped a handful of gold sovereigns on the bar and pushed them extravagantly towards the barmaid.

'Let's make a splash, Evie. Drinks for everyone.' He gestured at those pressed around him. 'Champagne if they like, so long as they drink a health to this young man.'

He gripped Jack tightly round the shoulders and with his free hand thrust a mug of beer at his face.

'Get this down, boy,' he ordered, as if it were medicine.

Jack was still staring, astonished, at the heap of sovereigns. The barmaid swept them up smartly without counting.

'Where'd you get all that money?' asked Jack, who never before had seen more than two sovereigns together.

'What?' asked Tony, lowering his head to Jack's level.

Jack tried to shout above the din. 'The money?'

'Mind your own business,' replied Tony. 'Happy birthday.'

He raised his own mug and turned to his new friends, eyes shining.

'Happy birthday to Jack!' he cried.

And everyone agreed.

Jack decided after the first gulp that he didn't like beer. It was thin and sour and, despite being liquid, somehow made his mouth dry. Soon, it was also doing unpleasant things to his stomach: swelling it to bursting point and beginning to give it cramps. But there was no escape. One pint followed another.

'Enjoy yourself! Enjoy yourself!'

With each mug planted in Jack's hand, his father's beaming face loomed larger in front of him. His breath became sourer than the beer itself; the bright, excited eyes became glazed. He began to sway and lurched to a seat against the wall, starting to talk loudly to a woman he'd never met.

Before Jack could decide whether he should join him, his stomach finally rebelled and forced its contents upwards. In a panic, Jack stumbled to the door and out into the street. There were people outside and, rather than be sick in front of them, he tottered as far away as he could before vomiting in the gutter.

He collapsed, clammy and cold, and instinctively clung on to the pavement as the world slowly revolved, like a tilting plate trying to tip him gently off. Jack managed to get to his knees, then his feet. Still the world revolved. He stood swaying, unsure where the Cap and Cockerel might now be and with a dread of returning to it. The mere thought of more beer made his gorge rise.

Jack staggered off down the street, using a wall to keep himself upright, then thought he recognized a turning that would lead home and aimed towards it. As he stepped into the road, he smelt warm horse then heard wheels and a great curse of alarm before something with legs knocked him over.

He lay in the revolving dirt and remembered the roof in Nunwell Street. Could he have been hit by a horse there too? Then he was sick again and knew the vomit hadn't missed his clothes this time. It didn't seem to matter. Someone was floating above him. Then someone else.

'Dear, oh dear,' said a voice. 'This won't do, will it.'

It was the second time Jack had woken up that night and he hadn't been to bed once.

This time he was in a room of some kind, with a stone floor. Neither his father's lodgings nor the Jevons' house had a stone floor. There was a horrible smell and his shirt was sticky. He realized the stickiness wasn't blood this time, just as he realized that the throbbing in his head had moved from the back to the front. He tried sitting up and was relieved that the stone floor didn't revolve. That was something. His thigh felt bruised. He remembered the cab driver's horse in the street.

'You stink.'

The voice made him jump. His eyes were becoming accustomed to the dark, helped by a pale light through what seemed to be a small square hole in a door. Someone was sitting hunched in the opposite corner of the room.

'You been sick twice.'

It was a girl's voice. She sounded disgusted rather than sympathetic. Jack could hardly blame her.

'I was on a roof,' he said, working his parched, foul-tasting mouth to see if he could still speak. 'In Nunwell Street. Because I heard a murder being planned. And I got hit on the head . . . Then my father took me to a pub.'

'Yes,' said the girl. 'Well the last bit's plain enough.'

'The rest's true as well,' protested Jack.

'Can you stand up?' The girl herself was on her feet now. She crossed to Jack and helped him to his feet. 'Only you'll be more comfortable not lying in your sick.'

She led him to the wall and sat him down again. Then she went to a bucket of water that Jack could hear rather than see and came back with a soaked cloth, which she wiped roughly down his face and chest. Jack gasped at the shock of cold water.

'Lean forward.'

He did as he was told and the girl swabbed his neck as well, before returning to the bucket for a fresh clothful and repeating the whole process.

'Can't drink the water now,' she said, 'but at least you'll smell better. Try and sleep. I don't think you'll puke no more.'

Jack leant back against the wall, not minding the clinging wetness of his shirt. He felt hollow and light-headed but refreshed.

'Where are we?' he asked suddenly.

'Clink, of course,' said the girl. 'A crusher brought you in.' She wasn't sure he'd understood so translated:

'We're in a cell. In a police station.'

Richard Featherstone woke suddenly at dawn, not on a stone floor but in his warm feather bed. He lay for a few moments, thinking of last night's supper party in his studio downstairs. His friends, mostly artists and models, had certainly enjoyed it, they'd stayed late enough, talking and laughing. The world of art, like the world of business, was buzzing with new ideas. He loved being part of it.

Richard got up and slipped into his dressing gown. Leaving his room, he paused on the landing and tapped at his father's bedroom door. There was no answer so he peeped inside. The bed hadn't been slept in.

Downstairs, the butler was emerging from the breakfast room. He showed no surprise at seeing Richard Featherstone so early. Though not as vigorous as his father, the son wasn't lazy.

'Good morning, Parfitt. Is my father about?'

'Uh, no, Mr Richard. As far as I'm aware, he didn't return home last night.'

'Oh.'

'Will you take breakfast downstairs, sir, or in your room?'

Richard ignored the question. 'There's been no word from my father?'

'Not that I've been informed, sir.' Parfitt paused politely then tried again. 'Breakfast, sir?'

'I think I'd better go and see that Pa's all right first,' said Richard.

He dressed quickly, while the carriage was brought round, and just half an hour later was in Nunwell Street. He'd brought a spare key and took it from his pocket, went quickly up the steps and turned it in the lock. The door didn't give; it was still bolted. Nobody answered his knock.

Richard hurried off to find a policeman and was in luck, meeting two of them at the first road junction. They recognized Henry Featherstone's son and returned with him to number seventeen.

'I'm concerned for my father,' said Richard as they walked. 'He may have been taken ill. We need to get into the building.'

The policemen briefly tried the door then regarded the ground-floor windows. They opted for the one without curtains, and with difficulty and a tear in his tailcoat, one of them climbed over the street railings. He peered in at the window then struck it once with his truncheon. Richard flinched as the glass shattered loudly. The policeman knocked out the jagged remnants and clambered through.

Within seconds Richard heard the bolts being drawn. He pushed in through the opening door, ahead of the second policeman.

'Where does he work, sir?' asked the policeman who'd broken in.

The closed office door was right beside them. Richard turned the handle and threw the door open.

'Pa . . .' he called. 'Are you . . .'

The words died away on his lips. The room looked like a battlefield. The portrait of his mother, the only painting his father cared for, hung at a crazy angle above the mantelpiece, its glass cracked. The dainty chair for visitors lay on its back, one leg snapped off, and even the heavy document cupboard had been toppled on its face. Piles of papers and files were strewn over the floor, most of them stained pink or red with blood. Blood was everywhere: splashed up the walls, across the floor, on the furniture and the curtains. And in the middle of the floor lay his father: a battered twisted heap, his unseeing eyes staring at the ceiling. For the first time in his life, Richard Featherstone screamed.

It took both policemen to pull him away. They forced themselves past him and into the room. Henry Featherstone had not succumbed without a struggle but he was most certainly dead. The gas lamps on the wall hissed on, regardless of the sudden daylight.

'There must be something going on,' said the girl in the police cell. 'Should have let us out by now.' She turned from the small barred window in the door for the umpteenth time. 'Gran'll be worried stiff.'

In the early morning light, Jack could see the concerned frown on her thin face. She sat down again. 'What's your family do?' she asked, clearly to take her mind off her gran.

'Haven't really got one,' replied Jack. 'Only my father now. He's a caretaker somewhere, I think.'

'My pa was a sewer hunter,' said the girl, whose name was April. 'Only he's dead now. Not in the sewers,' she emphasized. 'He died in his bed. So did Ma. So it's me and Gran now.'

She spoke with quiet determination, as if she were now head of the family, which Jack supposed she was.

'Why are you in here?' he asked.

'Got caught down a drain,' said April. 'I was in the sewers. I go down sometimes if there's no other work. Only it's a crime now, sewer hunting. So if the crushers spot you down there you get taken. Still, they give me bread and jam when they brung me in and I hid the shilling I'd just dug out the sewer mud, so I've done all right.'

'Won't you go to prison?'

'No, they'll just tell me off. You won't either. Not for being drunk. They'll just make you mop the floor in here then throw you out as well.' She got up and went restlessly to the door again. 'Gran'll be worried stiff,' she repeated as she peered through the bars. 'There must be something going on.'

There was.

Colonel Giles Radcliffe, Assistant Commissioner of the Metropolitan Police, had jumped from his carriage and was striding through the police station. He emerged into the assembly yard, and the sergeants and constables of E Division stood swiftly to attention under the watchful eye of their inspectors and station superintendent. Bigwig senior officers rarely visited police stations. Certainly not to take personal charge of murder investigations. And there was an added interest with this senior officer. He was only recently appointed, having returned from India, where he'd been Inspector General of the Bengal Police. It was rumoured he had 'ideas'. The rank and file of E Division weren't sure if that was a good thing or not.

The man from India addressed them without preamble.

'Good morning, gentlemen. I shan't detain you long. You will all know by now of the vile crime committed in Nunwell Street. The Impossible Crime, as the newspapers are already calling it, since there seems to have been no way in or out for the murderer: everything was still locked and barred after the event. Clearly, though, this crime was *not* impossible. Henry Featherstone is most certainly dead. He is also famous. His death will not go unregarded. The eyes of the nation are upon us, and the newspapers will ensure they remain so. That is both a burden and, I hope, an inspiration: an opportunity for the men of E Division to show their mettle. Between us we shall solve this "impossible crime", but we shall do so only by close attention to detail. No piece of information, however tiny, must be passed over. That is my method: neglect nothing; ignore nothing; dismiss nothing. If your sergeants or inspectors are too busy to listen, if you cannot find an officer of the Detective Branch, come straight to me. I am here to nail a murderer, not to stand on rank. Speak with me, work with me, and E Division will become as famous as Henry Featherstone himself.' He paused.

'We have so far only one possible lead: a reported sighting of a woman in Nunwell Street somewhere between seven and nine o'clock. We need more. Good luck.'

He nodded at the station superintendent and left the yard as swiftly as he'd entered.

A murmur passed through the massed policemen. In the very back row, Constable John Adams was feeling distinctly unsettled. Neglect nothing, ignore nothing, dismiss nothing. Dismiss nothing, that was the worrying one. He was thinking of the sweep's boy who'd accosted him in the street, claiming to have had a dream. Adams had dismissed *him*. Now the dream had proved truly prophetic. Perhaps he should mention it after all. To his sergeant, at least. To approach the Assistant Commissioner directly was unthinkable, despite the invitation to do so. Then again, what was the point? Adams had no idea who the boy was or where to find him, so mentioning it now would only cause trouble. Constable Adams didn't like trouble. It was probably just coincidence anyway.

'Anything wrong, Adams?'

'No, sergeant.'

'Get yourself out on the street then. Number five beat.'

'Yes, sergeant.'

April sprang back from the small barred window.

'Someone's coming at last.'

A key turned in the heavy lock and the door swung open.

'Out,' ordered the station sergeant. 'The pair of you.'

'What's happening?' asked Jack.

He'd never been in a police station before but, like April, he sensed heightened activity.

'No concern of yours, I hope,' said the sergeant. 'Go away and don't come back.'

Outside on the pavement, Jack said a slightly awkward goodbye to April. She looked very pinched and anxious in the daylight.

'Which way d'you go?' he asked.

April nodded to the right. 'Primrose Court, over Deptford.'

'I go this way,' said Jack, indicating left.

There was a brief pause.

'Stay off the beer,' advised April and she hurried away.

Jack walked more slowly. After a few minutes he realized he was heading towards the Jevons' address rather than his father's and reluctantly changed direction. He didn't know if his father would be indoors or not and wasn't in a hurry to find out. He still felt ill. He wiped his face again with the damp cloth that April had draped round his neck after washing him, and noticed that it was, in fact, a silk handkerchief. She hadn't asked for it back but he felt bad now that he hadn't returned it.

A news vendor was chanting enthusiastically at the corner of his father's street.

'Second edition. Financier found dead. Second edition. Grisly murder. Impossible crime . . .'

Jack's stomach lurched. Grisly murder? In his pocket he had a birthday sovereign given to him by his father and a single penny. He paid his penny for a paper and sat on the pavement to study it. He couldn't read well but was better at it than most sweeps' boys. His mother had taught him and the Jevons' house and yard were full of newspapers. Mr Jevons preferred the inside pages, where he found what he called 'gems of information'. Jack stared now at a front page.

Nunwell Street. Seventeen Nunwell Street. Violent Struggle. Bloody Murder. Doors and Windows Locked and Bolted. No Way In or Out. Mystery. Impossible Crime. Bloody Murder. MURDER. NUNWELL STREET!

Jack felt his skin crawling again and the now familiar rising within his stomach. He dropped the newspaper and rushed round the end of the houses and along the back alleyway to the shared privy, reaching it just in time before he was violently sick.

On his knees, shaking with nausea and shock, he confronted the truth. There had indeed been a killing.

And he knew where the murderer lived.

3

Lies

Richard Featherstone sat on the staircase. Number seventeen seemed full of policemen. They edged discreetly past him, up and down the stairs. He was still shaking and knew he must look awful. He could still hear his scream inside his head. Mercifully, his father's body had now been removed.

Inside the office to his left, the senior officer was going through his father's papers. An Assistant Commissioner, no less. Richard felt vaguely honoured on behalf of his father.

The Assistant Commissioner had first noted carefully where each of the documents that had fallen or been thrown from the desk was lying. Then he'd picked up every sheet and ledger with the greatest delicacy, as if they were in danger of disintegrating, peering at each one before laying it on the desk. He'd also read everything in a way that suggested the mysteries of finance, of stocks and shares and bonds and promissory notes, weren't mysteries at all. They were to Richard. He braced himself to feel foolish when the Assistant Commissioner asked him questions about his father's business.

'Did your father have enemies?'

It was, in the event, the obvious question.

Richard shrugged. 'I suppose for every investor who considered him a hero, there was one who did not.'

The Assistant Commissioner indicated the papers he'd been studying.

'This appears a most . . .' He chose the word carefully. '. . . ambitious venture. Were there partners in it? Sharing the risk?'

'Not that I know of. My father preferred to stand or fall alone.'

'Your mother . . .'

'Is in America. Visiting relatives.'

Mrs Featherstone had been visiting relatives for three years now. Both she and Richard's father had found their marriage pleasanter when apart.

'We shall need the names and addresses of all employees,' said the Assistant Commissioner. 'Everyone who was ever in this building, from the senior accountant to the cleaner.'

'I've already made details available to your men,' said Richard. 'Though I shouldn't like the lower staff . . . harrassed. My father was a generous employer. Well liked.' Richard looked at the Assistant Commissioner. 'I have a strong interest in the poor and middling, Colonel Radcliffe. They should not always be instinctively blamed. There are other motives for crime besides greed and envy.'

The Assistant Commissioner returned the look steadily.

'I do not establish guilt by instinct, Mr Featherstone. Only by fact.' He paused a moment. 'Who would you say knows this building best?'

When a neighbour came to use the privy, Jack was still slumped outside it.

'You're Tony Tolchard's boy, aren't you?' asked the neighbour.

Jack looked up and nodded.

'The crushers are at your door.'

Police Constable Downing was, in fact, inside the door now. Tony had tumbled out of bed at the third knock and let him in. They were sitting at the table when Jack eased into the room. His father was bleary-eyed and had clearly slept fully dressed but didn't look as if he'd been sick all night like his son.

'Seventeen Nunwell Street. You're the caretaker. Did you lock all the windows?' asked Constable Downing.

He seemed less than friendly, as if he'd taken an

instant dislike, which he had. He knew a boozy, good-for-nothing when he met one. He met a lot.

'Course I did,' said Tony comfortably.

'Look in every room before you left?'

Tony nodded again. 'That's my routine. There was no one in the building save Mr Featherstone and his son. Not even a mouse.'

He'd noticed Jack appear and grinned at him.

'Morning, son. Light the fire, will you, and put the kettle on? I'm sure the constable would like a cup of tea.'

The constable turned and looked at Jack, then frowned. He returned his gaze to Tony.

'Are you aware this lad spent last night in a cell? I picked him up off the street dead drunk.'

Tony shrugged. 'It was his birthday,' he said and grinned again, proudly. 'A young man's got to have such adventures.'

Jack crouched in front of the grate, fumbling with sticks and scraps of paper; and keeping his head down to hide his shock. He'd known his father was a caretaker. But not at number seventeen Nunwell Street. His stomach churned again but fortunately was now completely empty. He struck a lucifer with trembling fingers. As the small fire smouldered into life, he heard heavy footsteps on the stairs outside the room and a knock at the door.

Constable Downing went to open it and was startled to find the new Assistant Commissioner on the threshold. Richard Featherstone was behind him. Downing saluted and stood aside.

'Claims he shut and checked everything, sir, and was last out save Mr Featherstone junior.'

Colonel Radcliffe nodded and regarded Tony Tolchard, who'd remained seated casually, almost insolently, at the table. He also noticed the skinny boy by the fire.

'My son, Jack,' announced Tony, then, as Richard Featherstone entered the room, he stood up, suddenly a picture of grave condolence.

'Terrible news, Mr Richard.'

'Indeed, Tolchard. Thank you for your concern.'

The Assistant Commissioner seemed immediately to have lost interest in Tony and was wandering around the room, which was quite spacious, serving as kitchen, parlour and bedroom all in one.

'There will be no work for you today, of course,' continued Richard. 'And the office is closed until further notice, but you'll continue to be paid.'

Tony looked surprised.

'My father would have wanted it,' said Richard, 'and so do I. The tragedy's mine. It shouldn't inflict hardship on our employees. Here.' He took a card from inside his jacket and handed it to

Tony. 'My card. Come to the address on it for your wages from day to day until told otherwise. I'll arrange for the money to be given to you if I'm not there.'

Tony looked awkwardly at the card, hesitated as if about to speak, then put it in his pocket. Colonel Radcliffe noticed the hesitation. *He can't read*, he thought.

'You can also rest assured,' said Richard with a certain emphasis, 'that you will be treated fairly in these enquiries, and with respect.' He glanced at Constable Downing and the Assistant Commissioner. 'Colonel Radcliffe understands my views with regard to jumping to conclusions.'

'Thank you, sir,' said Tony humbly. 'Thank you very much.'

Colonel Radcliffe made no comment. 'How d'you come by so much money, Mr Tolchard?' he asked without turning.

A small heap of sovereigns lay on a low table beside the unmade bed. He was gazing down at them as he spoke, then turned with a look of mild enquiry.

Placing the kettle on its trivet on the grate, Jack was jolted by the echo of his own question in the Cap and Cockerel.

'I'm a gambling man, sir. Won it on the horses. Epsom last week.'

Jack's grip on the kettle tightened. His father

never gambled and despised those who did.

'Can you tell me where you were last evening? After leaving Nunwell Street?'

The Assistant Commissioner's voice was level, unthreatening, but Jack felt it would be a difficult voice to lie to. His father sounded unconcerned.

'Came home at six o'clock. Washed and changed. It was Jack's birthday. We went out to celebrate. At the Cap and Cockerel.'

'The boy was found in Branham Street at midnight, sir,' said Downing tersely. 'On his own.'

'There's a lady friend can vouch for me from midnight,' said Tony easily.

'And before?' asked Colonel Radcliffe.

'Why, as I've said: with Jack.'

'The entire evening?'

'The entire evening. We've been apart these past three years and more. Last night was precious to me. Ask the boy, if you like. He'll confirm what I say.'

'I wouldn't expect him to do anything else, Mr Tolchard.'

The Assistant Commissioner spoke as mildly as before but Jack remained rigid, still clutching the kettle. Another lie. They hadn't been together till well gone eight o'clock. Why was his father doing this?

The visitors didn't ask anything else. Jack stayed

where he was until they'd gone, then turned. Bewildered. Angry.

'Why did you say that, Father?' he demanded. 'I wasn't with you all evening. You know I wasn't. And the money. The gambling. You never –'

'Listen!' shouted his father, then he calmed visibly and spoke with great restraint, imparting wisdom. 'Listen, Jack. The crushers never believe the likes of us. Never. Not even when we're innocent. Especially when we're innocent. So you've always got to have a story, an alibi. You never tell them what they want to know. You never tell them anything. That's a lesson you'd better learn. And fast.'

A gaggle of neighbours had gathered in the road. Constable Downing shoved them away from the carriage as Richard Featherstone and Colonel Radcliffe climbed in. Richard eventually broke the silence as the carriage trundled away.

'So what is your opinion of Tolchard?'

Colonel Radcliffe shrugged non-committally. 'We shall see. He smelt of drink. Men who drink too much always betray themselves in the end. Liquor loosens the tongue.' He paused. 'I wonder, sir, if you would consider offering a reward for information?'

'So soon?' asked Richard, surprised. 'Surely those who have information can be trusted to come forward without money being dangled before their noses?'

Colonel Radcliffe made no comment.

Jack silently removed his vomit-stained clothes, making sure he took his gold sovereign from the trouser pocket, and put on his sweep's rags instead. Then he slung his sweep's sack over his shoulder and went downstairs.

Out in the backyard, he raised water from the pump into a bucket and plunged the dirty clothes in to soak. As he walked off through the alleyway, his father appeared from the house, clutching the small card Richard Featherstone had given him.

'Jack,' he called. 'Read this for me.'

Jack kept walking as if he hadn't heard. He didn't want to speak to his father right now. Couldn't, without asking him again about his lies.

He was drawn to Calborn Gardens. Perhaps being there again would help. Perhaps he'd remember more of the overheard conversation; something new, something vital he could tell the police without having to explain that his father had lied; that they hadn't been together for the whole of last night.

The Shoreys' house was at the end of the gracious terrace. A narrow side street flanked its side wall, and at the rear, at right angles to this, a backstreet ran the length of the terrace, with a high boundary wall enclosing the succession of small back gardens. Each property had its own back gate. The Shoreys' house, being at the end, also had a gate into its garden from the side street. Wrought-iron fire escapes, smartly painted, zigzagged down from attic level to basement scullery at the back of every house.

Calborn Gardens was empty. Its side street also. Jack found a section of the Shoreys' side garden wall with slight imperfections in its stonework and climbed it, strong fingers and toes clinging to the crevices. From there he climbed a drainpipe to the roof and crouched beside the chimney stack where he'd rested yesterday. He sat for some minutes thinking hard, but nothing new occurred to him.

Suddenly, he heard shouting. Jeering laughter and a stampede of feet. Looking down, he saw the Shoreys' son running into the side street. A gang of other schoolboys was pursuing him from Calborn Gardens. In panic, the tall, well-built but pale-faced boy rushed to the side gate and turned its handle. The gate wouldn't open. The ringleader of his tormentors called out to him.

'Now, now, Rupe, don't spoil the game. We only want to play.'

Rupert tugged and twisted more desperately at the handle. *Don't cry*, he pleaded with himself.

Please don't cry. But he knew he was going to. It was always them against him. He was always alone.

'Fight!'

Rupert heard a loud and urgent whisper somewhere above him.

'Turn round and fight.'

Rupert didn't believe in guardian angels.

'Fight!'

He looked up and saw the sweep's boy hanging from a drainpipe.

'Go on!' Jack jerked his free fist in demonstration of a right hook.

Rupert had never mastered the right hook in boxing lessons. He didn't even like hitting people. But he could hear the bullies close behind him now and he knew what game they wanted to play. It involved tearing his shirt and throwing his boots into distant gardens. He turned round blindly and swung his fist. The pain in his knuckles was awful as it connected but the shout from the ringleader, whose face he'd managed to punch, was quite unlike any sound he'd heard from him before. Rupert opened his eyes, saw blood, shock and sudden fear on the face in front of him, and windmilled forward, whirling his clenched fists like a machine and letting out what he was astonished to recognize as a savage roar. Some blows connected, most did not, but the battering was so violent and insistent and out of character that the bullies did what most bullies do when unexpectedly on the receiving end: they retreated. And when a skinny, ragged imp landed from nowhere beside the transformed Rupert, fists also clenched, they ran.

'I've opened the gate,' panted Jack. 'Come inside before the neighbours make a fuss.' And he pulled Rupert, whose arms were still involuntarily windmilling, backwards into the garden.

When the Rupert Shorey fighting machine finally ground to a halt and he turned to thank the sweep's boy, he'd disappeared. Rupert blinked and looked around and began to think he'd imagined the intervention, or that, possibly worse, it had indeed been supernatural. He hurried indoors and up to his room, avoiding the cook, the maid and his mother on the way. Upstairs he paused, calming himself down. His room overlooked the garden and the backstreet. He peered out. The sweep's boy wasn't in the garden or next door's garden, or the backstreet either. Was he on the roof? Rupert hurried from his room and along the corridor to the fire escape. He pushed open the door and stepped outside on to the metal landing.

Jack stifled a cry of surprise and jumped to his feet. He hesitated, not sure whether to bound up the iron staircase to the attic level or down towards the garden. Rupert was just as startled as he came face to face with his rescuer.

'So this is where you are,' he said, pointlessly, to cover his own nervous surprise. Then, as Jack moved to the flight of steps leading upwards: 'No. Please don't run away. I, um, want to thank you. For helping me down in the street.'

He wanted to say more but didn't know what.

Jack shrugged. 'That's all right.'

'I'm not quite as useless as I thought,' said Rupert. He tried to clench his fists again but they were already too stiff and swollen. He pretended they didn't hurt.

Jack shrugged again and smiled. 'You weren't what I'd call stylish but you gave them something to think about.'

'Yes,' said Rupert. 'I did, didn't I?' He smiled uncertainly, then quickly continued. 'Can I ask you a question? How did you do that yesterday? I saw you go up the chimney, and then you were on the roof. D'you turn into smoke or something?'

'I'll tell that secret,' said Jack, 'if you tell me who lives next door.'

'Next door? Why?'

'Just tell me.' Jack was no longer smiling.

Rupert hesitated. He owed this boy a lot but should he tell him about the neighbours?

'I'm not a thief,' Jack said sharply.

Rupert blushed. 'I didn't say you were,' he protested, but the sweep's boy had guessed correctly what was in his mind.

'I need to know,' said Jack, 'because of something I heard yesterday while I was up the chimney.' He hesitated. 'Something bad.'

Rupert stared at Jack's worried face and decided the boy was honest.

'The neighbours are Mr and Mrs Knight,' he said. 'But they've decamped to the country while the house is upside down.'

'Upside down?'

'Being painted. Well, when I say painted I don't mean decorated, I mean painted. By an artist. Mrs Knight's gone mad for murals, apparently. That's paintings on the wall: I didn't know either but Pa explained. It's frightfully expensive but they paint whatever you like: clouds, mountains, ships at sea –'

'So who *is* in the house?' interrupted Jack.

'Uh, the housekeeper. And one maid – the others have gone to the country. And the artist himself. Erskine his name is. He's got his own room, to mix up his paints and do his sketches and things.'

'Where?'

'Sorry?'

'Where's his room?'

'Next to mine. I've heard him through the wall.'

Jack sat and stared silently down through the grating of the fire escape, thinking hard. The voices had definitely come from the house next door, but which room? He tried to remember all the connecting flues inside the chimney and which way they went. In the end, he was certain.

'Will you tell me what you heard?' asked Rupert hesitantly. 'What was bad about it?'

Jack looked up. 'I heard voices in that room, the painter's room, planning a murder. At Nunwell Street.'

Rupert's mouth opened. He stared at Jack. 'Not *the* murder?'

Jack nodded. 'So I went to Nunwell Street last night. And I got hit on the head.'

Rupert could see the scabbing wound on the back of Jack's head. It looked extremely painful.

'You mean somebody bashed you? Gosh . . .!' It seemed an inadequate comment but it was all Rupert could manage.

'What's he like?' asked Jack. 'Erskine. Young? Old?'

'Quite young – and slim. Agile, I should think.' Rupert paused. 'D'you think he heard you in the chimney and followed you to Nunwell Street?'

Jack shook his head. 'I didn't go straight there. I wandered around and tried to speak to the police. And anyway, being agile doesn't mean you can climb on roofs. Especially in the dark.'

Rupert nodded. 'But,' he persisted, 'if Erskine and the person he was talking to realized they'd been overheard, you could be in danger, you know.'

Jack slowly looked up. This hadn't occurred to him. It wasn't a nice thought.

Rupert tried hard not to sound excited. This was shocking, dreadful. But rather thrilling too.

'What were you actually doing on the roof when you got hit?' he asked.

Jack told him about the loose tiles.

Rupert gave a long, low whistle.

'Suppose,' he said, 'suppose Erskine and his friend had made a hole earlier – under the tiles. Suppose they came back and found you crouching over it. Well, they'd bash you, wouldn't they? Especially if they realized you could have overheard them, being as how you're a sweep. I expect they meant to kill you.'

'Thanks,' said Jack, pretending he wasn't growing more afraid by the moment.

'I expect,' said Rupert, thinking it through, 'they made the hole bigger while you were knocked out, got through, killed Featherstone then got out of the same hole again and away. Did you look at the tiles when you woke up?'

Jack had to admit that he hadn't.

'I think you should,' said Rupert. Then he grinned, slightly embarrassed. 'Of course, that's easy for me to say.'

Jack raised his eyebrows and nodded. It certainly was. It wouldn't be this bubbling schoolboy taking the risk; it would be him.

'But as for right now,' resumed Rupert eagerly, 'I know he often goes out in the afternoons.'

'Who?'

'Erskine. Why don't we follow him? Or would you rather go to the police?'

'No,' said Jack hastily. 'No. Not yet.'

'What's he doing now?' whispered Constable Adams, who'd been reassigned from his beat to assist in Nunwell Street. He and Constable Downing were in the hallway of number seventeen, peeping into Henry Featherstone's office. The Assistant Commissioner was on his hands and knees, peering up the chimney.

'This is what he does, apparently,' muttered Downing, half impressed, half deeply sceptical. 'Clues.'

'Why not just bring in the caretaker and give him a proper pumping?' asked Adams. 'Then work his way up through the clerks and accountants. It's obvious: someone's had their hand in the till. Guv'nor's twigged. Got bashed for his trouble. Obvious.'

He knew it wasn't obvious at all, but saying it kept at bay his nagging worry about the sweeping boy and the dream.

Downing merely shrugged.

Colonel Radcliffe was aware the men were watching him. He didn't mind. The world was changing and the world of crime with it. New habits of detection needed to become ingrained. Example was the best teacher.

He turned again to the bloodstains. There were many of them; now dried. On the floorboards, on the desk, the wall, a chair. The chair was the most interesting. It was the only dainty item in a room of sparse heavy furniture. It had been broken in the struggle. Someone had touched it with blood on their hands. Possibly Featherstone himself. Possibly the murderer.

Colonel Radcliffe touched it himself now, carefully lifting one of its splintered legs between his fingertips and propping it on the window sill where it caught the light. He peered once more at its bloody marks.

'There he goes!' cried Rupert.

They were watching from the window of his room. Jack, standing beside Rupert on a sheet of newspaper to catch any soot from his clothes, saw a youngish man in a long coat, wide-brimmed hat and yellow scarf swirl down the back garden path.

The man opened the gate and strode away along the backstreet with a parcel under his arm.

'Come on,' said Rupert excitedly and he hurried from the room. Jack hesitated then followed.

'Rupert?' Mrs Shorey's surprised voice came rather querulously up the stairs.

Rupert halted abruptly and turned.

'Go down the fire escape,' he hissed at Jack. 'I'll meet you in the street.'

Jack flitted away just in time before Rupert's mother appeared.

'What are you doing home at this time?' she asked, frowning at her son.

'Forgot my prep,' said Rupert quickly. 'Old Fergie sent me home for it. Just fetching it now.'

He ran back to his room, grabbed the first book he could find and ran out again.

'Bye, Ma.' He attempted to bustle downstairs past her.

'What on earth have you done to your hands?' Mrs Shorey stared appalled at the swollen red bundles of finger.

'Just fighting,' replied Rupert, as if it were his regular pastime. He clattered away towards the front door.

Mrs Shorey was too surprised to call him back. She wandered suspiciously into his room. And was further disconcerted by the grubby sheet of newspaper by the window.

Jack was already in the backstreet behind Calborn Gardens. He turned as Rupert puffed up behind him. For some reason Rupert was clutching a book.

Erskine was disappearing round the next corner. He was walking swiftly. It was hard to keep up and out of sight at the same time, but fortunately he didn't look back.

After about five minutes, he turned into what seemed to be a muddy dead end, a truncated roadway in which his way was barred by huge wooden hoardings. But Erskine seemed to know what he was doing. He squeezed between two of the hoardings and disappeared again.

Jack and Rupert ran to the great wooden wall and peered through the narrow gap. Below them was a vast trench gouged out of the earth. And from the trench rose up a great latticework of steel girders and scaffolding, and the beginnings of brick retaining walls. A new railway cutting and a bridge.

Erskine was clearly visible, his yellow scarf distinctive amongst the drab clothes of the workmen on the site. No one took any notice of his approach; certainly no one challenged him.

He climbed a ladder and perched on a wide crosspiece, a long way above the ground, which braced the scaffolding on either side. Once settled, he unwrapped his parcel, which contained a large pad of paper, and began to draw, sketching the scene around him and the men labouring within it.

'We need to get closer,' said Jack. 'I want to see him properly, so I'll recognize him.'

He and Rupert slipped between the hoardings and quickly ran down the slope of churned earth towards the nearest end of the scaffolding. Erskine, safe on his perch, was talking intently to a workman, a scaffolder erecting the next level of latticework above him. The scaffolder stepped confidently back and forth across the gaps between the narrow girders, balancing effortlessly despite the heavy metal bolts he was carrying.

'Stay here,' said Jack, and he slipped away from Rupert, in amongst the poles and planks and ladders, then began to climb.

It was far easier than a drainpipe, let alone a chimney. Like scaling a tall tree on which all the branches were straight and sturdy. He was soon level with the scaffolder and looking down on Erskine himself.

'Oi! What's your game?'

A foreman had spotted Jack and yelled at him.

'Out of it! Scarper!'

Jack scarpered. But not before Erskine had looked up and seen him.

He was an observant man and noted every detail, from Jack's bare feet to his ragged sweep's clothing.

4

The Grapnel

Jack and Rupert scrambled back up to the wooden hoardings, squeezed through and kept running, though nobody seemed to be chasing them. Eventually they stopped. Rupert was enjoying the adventure immensely, even though he was out of breath.

'Well!' he said. 'That was interesting.'

Jack had got a good look at Erskine's face. Beyond that, he wasn't sure they'd achieved much. And Erskine had got an equally good look at him.

'He's quite big,' he said. 'I don't see how he could have been in the roof valley without me seeing him. And I would definitely have heard him climbing over from the next.'

'You might not have heard that scaffolder. The one he was talking to. Did you see the way he was balancing? I bet he could sit on top of a church spire and eat his lunch.'

Jack liked to think he could too, given the

chance, and felt a slight pang of irritation. What did Rupert know about such things?

'You *must* go back to the roof now,' urged Rupert. 'If there *is* a proper hole under those tiles, we'll have solved the impossible crime.'

We? thought Jack.

'Let's meet again tonight, shall we?' Rupert suggested. 'When you've been to Nunwell Street. How about eight o'clock on the fire escape?'

'So how's that handsome young man of yours today?'

The barmaid handed Tony another pint of beer as she enquired. They'd discussed the murder and agreed it was dreadful. Evie was ready for a more cheerful topic.

'Oh, fine, fine,' chuckled Tony.

He was enjoying the freedom to be in the Cap and Cockerel in the afternoon; to be unemployed yet still paid. He'd forgotten to bring the card that Richard Featherstone had given him. Evie could read. But he'd see Jack again this evening and smooth things over. In the meantime, he still had a last few sovereigns to get through. He laughed happily.

'He did it proper. Crushers picked him up in the street, sick as a dog. Spent the night in a cell.'

'Chip off the old block then, eh?'

'Absolutely,' agreed Tony, missing the irony.

'Absolutely. Clever too. Can read y'know. Oh yes. And wonderful bold. Climb anything. I'm going to put him to a proper trade. Put him on the buildings, probably. Or the railways, the new stations and tunnels and suchlike. There's money there. Good money. Put a stop to this chimney-sweeping nonsense.'

He emptied his mug and pushed it back towards Evie for another refill. 'Have one yourself,' he said, fishing the sovereigns from his pocket.

'Still flush then?' observed Evie, taking the coin he offered.

Tony slipped the rest back into his pocket. 'A little deal I did,' he said, and winked at her as she handed him his pint. 'Private like.' He chuckled and took another long drink.

Unnoticed behind him, a man in a large hat and coat listened to the talkative caretaker.

Nunwell Street was not as deserted as the last time Jack had been there. Far from it. A cordon of policemen at either end held back curious sightseers; hopeful journalists waited eagerly for any scrap of information they might be thrown. Other policemen were meticulously searching not just the railed frontage of every building in the street, but also the pavement and even the street gutters. Jack kept well back but still heard the respectful, whispering hush as the bystanders saw

Richard Featherstone emerge from number seventeen and get into his carriage.

Gradually, towards dusk, the crowds thinned and finally only the policemen were left. A sergeant dismissed all but three of them and one of these positioned himself outside the front door of the dead man's office.

Jack made his way unseen to the drainpipe at the back that he'd used the night before. From there he climbed stealthily across the roof ridges to the valley above number seventeen.

It wasn't as late or as dark as on his previous visit and he was able to see the broken tile quite clearly as he eased himself down towards it. But visibility brought disappointment. The tile he'd stumbled on and the loose ones around it hid no secret: there was no hole beneath them. No one had climbed down through the roof into Featherstone's office.

Jack turned away and began to retrace his careful steps. Then, as he did so, he noticed something else. Something lodged in the wide gutter at the rear of the building. He slithered quickly down towards it.

Too quickly. Sudden voices down in the lane behind Nunwell Street alarmed him. He knew he'd made a noise, and froze. After a few seconds, he peeped over then ducked down flat again. The two patrolling policemen were in the lane. Looking up towards him. Jack stayed still. He heard their boots and then the sharp rap of a doorknocker across the lane. Peeping over again, Jack saw the caretaker of the building opposite open the door a crack and peer out at the policemen.

'Sorry to trouble you, sir. Could we possibly have a look out of your top-floor window?'

They wanted to look across. They would see him. The find that Jack had scrambled down to was now almost touching his nose. It was hard and metallic, with a narrow shaft and iron hooks. A grapnel. When he heard the policemen go indoors, he quickly picked it up. The iron hooks were neatly hinged and when Jack squeezed them they folded flat against the shaft. He slipped the grapnel into his sack and crept away towards the drainpipe, low and swift as a spider.

Constable Downing gazed across at the empty roof of seventeen Nunwell Street.

'Not even a pigeon,' he grunted at Constable Adams beside him. 'You're hearing things.'

Adams shrugged. 'Better tell the Colonel anyway. Ignore nothing, remember?'

Downing grunted again.

Colonel Radcliffe was pleased. He congratulated them both on their diligence. But that was the end of it. He'd already examined the roof space of number seventeen himself. Crawled beneath the rafters for evidence of entry from above.

There was none. And none in the adjoining walls of numbers fifteen and nineteen. It was a favourite trick of patient burglars to bore through party walls. But not this time. No one had come at Featherstone from next door, any more than they'd come at him through the roof.

Slowing down when well away from Nunwell Street, Jack listened to a church clock chiming. Seven. Still an hour before the rendezvous with Rupert. He thought of the girl in the cell, April, her rough kindness and undernourished face. Her silk handkerchief was soaking in the bucket in his father's backyard with the rest of Jack's clothes. It was probably ruined. He still felt guilty about it. And he had his birthday gift, his father's sovereign, in his pocket. He headed for London Bridge and Deptford.

He found Primrose Court eventually. There were no primroses, just dirt and suspicion and listless faces lolling around crowded doorways.

Nobody spoke but someone pointed him towards a house at the end of the court with more paper and rags in the windows than glass. A padding ken, the lowest of low lodging houses, where a bed, or a share of one, could be had for twopence a night.

The proprietor bellowed upstairs and April appeared. She didn't seem pleased to see Jack.

'What d'you want?'

Jack shrugged awkwardly. He felt he was intruding. 'To pay you back. For being kind last night.'

He held out the sovereign, half expecting her to refuse, but her fingers snatched and closed over it like a bony little trap. She didn't say thank you.

Jack couldn't help his eyes flickering around the dismal, threatening surroundings. His life was hard but not this hard. People brushed past him, in and out, giving him glances as if assessing his value. He wasn't worth robbing now he'd parted with the sovereign, and he hoped they could tell.

'Mostly thieves here,' said April matter-of-factly, as if reading his thoughts. 'But it ain't so bad. Only fifteen bodies in our room, and me and Gran have a bed to ourselves.'

Jack nodded. 'Wish her well for me.' There seemed nothing else to say. He made to leave.

'You was right then. You did hear murder being planned.'

Jack stopped and turned, surprised that she remembered what he'd said in the cell.

'Yes.'

'Or was that how you got your bang on the head – when Featherstone put up a fight?'

Jack was shocked. 'You can't think I did it?'

April shrugged. 'There's enough in here who'd

65

have been glad to. There's rumours there was money in his desk.'

Jack stared at her fist, still clenched round the gold coin; the one of many gold coins suddenly in his father's possession.

'Who says that?' he demanded sharply. 'I've not heard it.'

April merely shrugged again. 'Who knows who ever starts a rumour? What you got in there?' She'd noticed the sack.

'The thing I was hit with, I think. It was on the roof.' He glared at her. 'But what's it to you? If you think I did the murder?'

He turned to leave but she tugged his shirt.

'Course I don't. You could never have done for Featherstone. He'd have wiped the windows with you. Show me.'

She nodded at the sack. Jack relented, but as he took it from his shoulder April stopped him and glanced round warily.

'Not in here, though,' she said and walked out past him, heading towards the river.

The tide was out and the muddy beach glistened in the fading twilight.

'Tread where I tread,' instructed April. 'There's quicksand.'

Jack followed cautiously. If she didn't already have his sovereign, he'd have suspected she was planning to rob him.

When she felt she was far enough from eavesdroppers, April stopped.

'Now show me.'

Jack took his find from the sack. April turned it over in her hands. The hooks were still folded flat against the shaft. She flicked her wrist and the hooks sprang open, like an umbrella.

'Bet you don't know what it is,' challenged Jack.

'It's a grapnel,' said April simply. 'I've seen them at the docks. You think this is what hit you?'

'Yes, but I don't think there was anyone else on the roof holding it.' He was eager to explain now. 'I think it was thrown. From the ground.'

'What, thrown at you deliberately?'

'Maybe not. Maybe that was just my bad luck.'

'So why else would anyone have thrown it?'

'I don't know that either. But there's a first-floor window at the back, directly under where I found this.'

'The windows were all locked, though,' said April. 'According to the newspapers.'

Jack dug a big toe into the cool mud.

'Yes,' he agreed, deflated. 'So this proves nothing.'

There was a brief pause. April gave him a sidelong, rather calculating glance. 'Windows can be locked from the outside,' she said with a shrug.

'What?' Jack was startled.

'So I've heard.'

'How? How's that possible?'

April didn't reply. Instead, she asked: 'Will there be a reward? He was rich, so his family must be too.'

'I don't know,' said Jack. It had never occurred to him.

'But if we could find out who did it,' continued April, 'and tell his son, he'd give us a lot of money, surely. He ought to.'

Jack looked at her. 'He might, I suppose.'

He paused then put the grapnel back in the sack.

'I have to show this to someone else. D'you want to come?' He looked up again. 'You might get some food.'

Although being underground in a sewer held no terrors for April, Jack could soon tell she was afraid of heights. The garden wall in Calborn Gardens wasn't that high, but by the time he'd helped her to the top of it she was trembling and her breathing was shallow. She clung to the coping stones like a limpet while Jack jumped down into the garden.

'Lower yourself down, then drop,' he whispered. 'I'll catch you.' Nothing happened. 'April, hurry.'

There was a whimper and scrabbling above,

then she fell on top of him. But she picked herself up quickly and shook herself free, too proud to take his offered hand.

Jack led the way to the fire escape. April paused for a moment, staring down at the warm firelight in the basement as they crept past, and breathing in the smell of proper food baking. She thought of the very different Primrose Court and hoped her gran was safely asleep.

Rupert was waiting anxiously at the top of the iron stairs.

'Who's this?' He stared at the newcomer.

'April,' said Jack. 'I met her in a police cell.'

'Gosh . . . You'd better come inside.'

Rupert ushered Jack and April into the passageway then closed the fire-escape door behind them.

'Shush now,' he whispered, and hurried softly along the carpeted corridor. Jack and April followed. Rupert showed them into his room and closed the door. April just stood a moment, overwhelmed by the opulence and cleanliness of a schoolboy's room. All this for one person.

Rupert had taken the precaution of spreading newspaper again.

'I hope you don't mind,' he said, rather embarrassed, indicating for his visitors to sit on it. 'Only Ma doesn't miss a thing. I'll clear it away when you've gone.'

Jack and April didn't mind. They sat on the newspaper, April still staring about her.

Rupert perched on the chair by his desk and leant forward eagerly.

'Did you get on the roof?' he asked Jack.

'Yes. But your idea was wrong. There's no big hole, no damage at all under the tiles. Even the scaffolder couldn't have got in that way.'

'Oh.'

For a moment Jack took a mean little satisfaction in Rupert's disappointment then chided himself for it.

'But I found this in the gutter.' He pulled it from the sack and gave April an acknowledging glance. 'It's called a grapnel. We think it's how the murderer got in, but we haven't worked it out properly yet.'

We this, we that. It sounded to Rupert as if Jack and the girl were bowling happily along without him. He tried not to look even more hurt.

'See this?' Jack was pointing at an iron ring at the end of the grapnel shaft. 'A rope could have gone through here – not tied in a knot, just threaded like cotton through a needle, so when he'd finished he could pull it out again and leave no sign.'

'Sign of what?' asked Rupert.

'The rope. The murderer could have thrown the grapnel so it stuck in the gutter . . . The rope threaded through this ring here would have hung down to the ground. Then it would have been easy as anything to climb up the rope to a window.'

'What window?'

'There's one at the back on the first floor,' said Jack. 'Then, when he climbed down again, all he had to do was pull the rope out.'

'But what about the grapnel?'

'He wouldn't have worried about it. No one would be able to see it from the ground.'

Rupert screwed up his face. Jack wondered for a moment if he didn't understand or was just being difficult because it wasn't his idea. It was neither.

'But surely that thing wouldn't hold a man's weight,' objected Rupert.

'Come outside and I'll show you.' Jack jumped up, determined to prove his theory.

Rupert reached the door before him and peeped out of the room. He nodded and they padded quickly and quietly along the passage to the fire escape. Outside, bright moonlight silvered the rooftops and the fire escape itself. Jack removed the frayed length of thin cord he wore wrapped a couple of times round his waist as a belt and threaded it through the iron ring. He hitched his trousers up hard. They felt a bit loose round his middle and he hoped they wouldn't fall down.

He stared up at the roof then down again at the grapnel in his hands.

'My belt's not long enough to reach from here,' he whispered, and trotted up the next flight of iron stairs to the attic level.

Rupert and April stared up after him. They watched him lean back against the iron railing, arm outstretched, then deftly toss the grapnel upward. Its metal hooks glinted in the moonlight as it arced into the sky, and the cord trailed for a moment like a kite tail. The hooks clattered briefly but noisily on the slates before sliding and sticking fast in the gutter.

'Ssshhh!' Rupert was aghast. They all stood quite still for a whole minute but no parent appeared to demand what was going on.

Jack had to jump to catch hold of the two dangling ends of cord. He grabbed them and tugged hard, testing that the grapnel was firmly lodged, then hauled himself hand over hand up the cord, with his feet braced against the house wall.

'See,' he whispered down at Rupert. 'It would hold an elephant.'

'I believe you. Now come down.'

Jack hadn't finished his experiment yet.

'Imagine this is the back wall in Nunwell Street,' he continued.

Rupert nodded anxiously. April wasn't anxious

for Jack. She just wished she too could hang like a spider on a thread.

Jack climbed a little higher. It wasn't exactly like Nunwell Street. There the grapnel had caught directly above a window. Here the nearest window, the attic window, was some way to his left. He swung the rope from side to side like a clock's pendulum, reaching out with his foot until he could gain a hold on the sill.

'Don't fall,' pleaded Rupert.

Jack smiled to himself. The gutter was solid. There was no danger of falling. He had both feet on the window sill now and, taking his weight on his toes, he jerked the cord so that the grapnel moved along the gutter and he could hang directly in front of the glass.

It was a sash window. Like those at Nunwell Street. To open it you had to pull the bottom pane upwards until it slid behind the top pane. Holding on to the grapnel cord with one hand, Jack tried with the other to raise the sash. It wouldn't budge. He gripped the sill even harder with his toes, tied his cord under his armpits to support him, and heaved again with both hands. Still nothing happened. Something was pressing down, preventing any upwards movement at all. Despite April's jibe about him being used for wiping windows, Jack knew he was no weakling. A grown man would have had no more success.

Entry was impossible without breaking the glass.

'Someone's coming!' Rupert's whisper was loud and urgent. 'I think it's Erskine!'

'Scarper, Jack!' hissed April. 'Quick!'

Jack heard two sets of feet scampering back indoors somewhere beneath him. There wasn't time for him to shuffle the grapnel back along the gutter to the fire escape. Instead, he pulled himself up the cord hand over hand and scrambled on to the roof, just as the artist let himself into next door's garden through the back gate. It was a rare clear night and the garden was peaceful. Erskine looked up appreciatively at the brilliant stars and shining disc of moon. He paused. There was something on the roof. Crouched against a chimney. Or was it *somebody*? For a moment Erskine thought it was the sweep's boy from the railway site, but the creature slid silently out of view behind the chimney, moving as gracefully and stealthily as a cat. Erskine stared for a few moments more then closed and locked the gate and went indoors.

When he had gone, Jack quickly unhooked the grapnel and descended by the drainpipe.

'You were right. It was Erskine,' he said as he slipped into Rupert's room.

'He didn't see you, did he?' asked Rupert, worried for Jack but for himself too. This was developing into a bit too much excitement so close to home.

'I don't think so.' Jack wasn't sure but there was nothing he could do about it. He changed the subject.

'D'you believe us now about the grapnel?' he asked. 'And can you see how the murderer got to the window?'

'Yes.' Rupert nodded.

'Good. But what *I* can't see,' said Jack, 'is how he got in *through* the window. And out again.'

Rupert was rather glad. It seemed it hadn't all been worked out without him after all.

'But that's why April's here,' continued Jack. He turned to where she was sitting on the newspaper.

April stared silently back at him, a slight, challenging smile on her pinched face.

'You can't expect a share of the reward if you don't help,' said Jack determinedly.

'What reward?' asked Rupert.

April looked defiantly up at him. 'I'll need a cheese wire,' she said. 'One with a bit of cheese on it would be nice.'

Rupert frowned at her then left the room and crept downstairs. His parents were in the drawing room. Cook, he knew, would be in her own room now, which left Elizabeth in the kitchen. He rang the bell in the front parlour then darted out and hid in the passage until Elizabeth, summoned by the bell, hurried by. Rupert emerged, ran to the kitchen, grabbed the cheeseboard from the larder and dodged out again before Elizabeth, muttering under her breath, returned.

April consumed a large piece of cheddar before saying another word. Then she unfastened the cheese wire from its retaining screw on the board and stood up.

'We need a window,' she said, then nodded at Jack. 'And you'll have to go outside again, of course.'

Rupert led the way up the attic stairs, lit the gas lamp in the attic room and closed the door behind them. Jack hurried to the window that had refused to open for him earlier and, grasping the brass finger holds at the bottom, tried to lift it. It moved only the merest fraction, and instantly he saw why. Screwed to the window sill was a short metal post with a horizontal bar on top. The bar, which pivoted on its post, had been pushed right across towards the glass and was now wedged on top of the window frame itself. The window was securely locked.

'It's a bit rusty,' observed April critically. 'Does it open?'

She seized the brass knob on top of the bar and pulled it. The bar swivelled away from the window frame. April slid the sash easily upwards and cool night air flowed into the room. 'Well, that's a start,' she said.

Both boys watched intently while April deftly looped the cheese wire round the brass knob on the locking bar, then trailed both ends out over the sill and left them dangling outside.

'Go outside, close the window then pull both the wires,' she said to Jack.

'Pull them?'

April nodded. 'Gently. Don't tug till it's tight, then tug one end hard. Only one end.'

Jack left the other two in the attic room and went out on to the fire escape. The window was a long way to his left. It wasn't going to be easy to reach it without the grapnel and rope, but using those would mean making more noise and he knew they'd made enough already. He climbed on to the sloping handrail of the fire escape and, with hands spread on the house wall, edged sideways as close as he could get to the window. Bracing himself, and trying not to think of the long drop to the basement if he should slip, he stretched up, clawed at the bottom of the window sash and pulled it down shut. Now he had to grope around on the sill for the gossamer-thin strands of cheese wire. He wound both ends round his fingers and pulled gently. At first, nothing happened, but as he maintained the gentle pressure he felt resistance on the other side of the window. The wire looped round the knob was pulling the bar back towards the glass. He pulled harder and heard a click.

Above him, April loomed inside the window, gesturing with her hands, but Jack didn't need telling what to do. He let go of one end of the wire and tugged the other end hard. The wire slid silently out from under the window frame.

Inside, Rupert stared open-mouthed at the disappearing cheese wire.

'It's locked!' he exclaimed. 'He locked it with the wire . . .' He tapped excitedly on the window, peering out at Jack. 'You pulled the lever across. Click!' His exultant expression changed. 'Jack! Are you all right?'

Jack wasn't all right. His feet were slipping and he was about to fall.

The window flew up and Rupert leant out and seized an arm. Beside him, April managed to grab a handful of Jack's shirt. Between them, they hauled him up over the window sill into the attic.

April glanced out of the window then slid it shut. 'You'd have made a real mess of the rose beds,' she remarked.

Jack got to his feet, feeling slightly annoyed at having needed the rescue.

'That's how the murderer did it then,' he said, almost dismissively.

April shrugged. 'It's how to get out of a window and leave no trace,' she said calmly. 'Or so I've heard.' She paused. 'But you can't *unlock* a window from the outside.'

She looked at Jack and her cool certainty sank into his heart. Mind your own business, his father had told him when Jack had asked about the heap of sovereigns on the pub bar. Was this where the money had come from? Had he been paid to leave a window unlocked?

'What's the matter, Jack?' asked Rupert.

Jack looked up miserably and shook his head. 'Nothing.'

5

Suspects

The journalist was shown into the Assistant Commissioner's office. He was from the *London News*. He smiled a trifle smugly.

Colonel Radcliffe didn't much like journalists. Their interest in crime was purely financial. It sold newspapers. Whenever offering to help the police, they were invariably helping themselves. He wished he hadn't agreed to the interview.

'You'll pardon me for calling on you so late, Colonel, but I wonder if you could tell us about Freda Barlow.'

Colonel Radcliffe stared at the smiling journalist. It had been a long day and he was tired.

'Freda Barlow?' repeated his visitor. 'Widow of Edwin Barlow? Fellow who hanged himself a few days ago. Up to his eyes in debt. It was in the newspapers.'

'Everything is in the newspapers,' remarked Colonel Radcliffe sourly. 'Not all of it is true.'

'Well, this is true enough, sir. Freda Barlow was

seen by a dozen people shouting at Henry Featherstone yesterday.'

Radcliffe looked blank and the journalist's smile broadened. It was so sweet to be one up on the police.

'At the Prince's Bridge ceremony? She as good as threatened him for misleading investors. Her husband amongst them. You weren't aware of this?' He took out his notepad. 'May I assume then that you haven't followed it up?'

Radcliffe looked at him sharply. 'You may assume nothing.'

The journalist was writing quickly as he spoke.

'Have you asked the witness who saw a woman in Nunwell Street if he recognizes Mrs Barlow as that woman?'

'The witness who *claims* to have seen a woman,' corrected Colonel Radcliffe stiffly.

'Of course.' The journalist had sat down without being invited. He leant back in his chair and regarded the Colonel. 'We, that is to say, the *London News*, being, unlike yourself, aware of Mrs Barlow's views on Henry Featherstone, arranged for the witness to call at her house a short while ago.' His eyes narrowed. 'He positively identified her as the woman he saw in Nunwell Street. May we have a comment, sir, on this latest and significant development?'

*

Rupert was the proud owner of a magnifying glass. It had been a gift from his mother, who had hoped to encourage in him an interest in natural history. She vaguely felt that if her son was to be absent from school so often, he might educate himself a little by studying insect life in the garden. This hadn't worked, however, because nature was at its most abundant in summer and Rupert was then indoors with pretended hay fever.

Rupert did like the idea, though, and fancied he looked rather intelligent, examining things through the glass and nodding. He was doing it now, in his room, where he and Jack and April were still secretly gathered. His subject was the grapnel.

'You can see blood on this hook,' he said. 'And just a little hair.'

He looked up consideringly at Jack, who was leaning beside him, then, without asking, reached up and tugged at Jack's head.

'Ow!'

'Sorry,' said Rupert, not sounding it.

He held the couple of hairs he'd pulled from Jack's scalp under the glass, close to the grapnel hook.

'Same colour,' he said confidently. 'This is definitely what hit you. Unintentionally, I expect. I mean, if they'd seen you on the roof, they would hardly have drawn your attention by throwing the grapnel, would they? I think it was an accident. They didn't know you were up there. They didn't know they'd hit you. The grapnel clunked off your head then stuck fast in the gutter where they wanted it, so they just carried on as planned. Erskine might not have managed a roof but I bet he could manage a window – and so could his scaffolder, of course.'

'Rupe? Why is your lamp still on?'

Mrs Shorey's voice was on the floor below but sounded likely to come rapidly closer.

'Out! Out!' whispered Rupert desperately. He shoved the grapnel into its sack and pushed it under his bed, then started scrabbling up newspaper from the floor.

'Meet you again tomorrow?' asked Jack.

'Where, where?'

'Come to Jevons' yard, Redbarn Road. It's safer. There's a flat roof round the back – across the lane. Ten o'clock?'

Rupert nodded. Jack and April darted out into the passage and headed for the fire escape.

'D'you trust that Rupert?' asked April as she and Jack hurried away from Calborn Gardens.

She didn't say much, so when she spoke Jack paid attention.

'Yes,' he said, surprised. 'Why not?'

April shrugged. 'He's rich.'

'Not that rich, I don't think,' said Jack. 'And

what does it matter if he is? Doesn't mean we can't trust him.'

'He kept the grapnel,' said April. 'It's the only thing you'd got. The only evidence.'

'So?'

'So he lives next door to the artist man. The one you think you heard planning the murder. Perhaps they're friends.'

Jack didn't speak for several seconds.

'He'll be at the meeting place tomorrow,' he said at last. 'I'm sure of it.'

They parted and Jack made his way home, bracing himself for the questions he must ask about the window at the back of Nunwell Street. The window that someone must have left unlocked before the murderer arrived.

His father was snoring loudly. Dead drunk. Unwakeable. When it came to it, Jack was relieved.

Rupert had lain in bed awake all night, his mind spinning with grapnels and ropes and window locks. He'd got into minor trouble for the cheeseboard but his mother had found nothing else amiss.

By breakfast time he was forming a plan. Since his Jack-inspired victory over the bullies, he thought of himself as a bolder person than before; capable of being resourceful in areas other than avoiding school. Before going downstairs to breakfast, he made his silent way towards his father's library. History had always been his favoured subject but he knew there was also a whole shelf of weighty books on art.

Fortunately, there was still some food left when he did reach the breakfast room.

'Why aren't you ready for school, sir?'

The familiar question received an unfamiliar answer.

'Holiday, Pa.'

'Oh. Well, you get far too many.' Mr Shorey grunted and returned his attention to his newspaper.

Rupert didn't say that if it hadn't been a holiday he'd have been on his way by now, ready to seek out the bullies and give them another bashing. But there were other excitements in store today. He shovelled on the marmalade.

'I see a woman's been named,' said his father. 'A Mrs Barlow. Her husband hanged himself because of debt. Definitely identified as the woman seen in Nunwell Street. I told you it was someone who'd got their fingers burnt, didn't I?'

'Did you, dear?' said Mrs Shorey. 'Yes, I expect you did.'

'Can I see, Pa?' asked Rupert.

'Certainly not,' replied his father. He held the newspaper closer.

Rupert returned to his heavily laden toast, but his overactive mind had been shooting off in all directions during the night. Regrettable suspicion was niggling at him again.

'Pa,' he asked, 'could someone have climbed into Mr Featherstone's office down the chimney? From the roof?'

'I can't see a woman doing that,' scoffed his father dismissively.

Rupert didn't mean a woman; he meant a skinny sweeping boy.

'No, dear,' said his mother calmly. 'Not from outside. Chimney pots are far too narrow. And I believe there was a fire burning in the grate at the time of the murder.'

'Oh,' said Rupert, suddenly ashamed. 'Thanks, Ma.'

Mr Shorey stared at his unexpectedly knowledgeable wife and kept his ignorance to himself.

'Pa?'

'*Yes*. What now?'

'I've been reading a lot about paintings. You know: art. It's awfully interesting. I was wondering, as we've got a real artist living next door at the moment, d'you think you could make an appointment for me to visit him and, well, discuss his work?'

Mr Shorey laid aside his newspaper, stunned.

'Discuss his work?'

'Well, you know, at least look at it. I think it would be a fine opportunity for me. Frightfully educational.'

There was a brief silence while Mrs Shorey smiled at her husband.

'You see, Desmond?' she said, as if vindicated in some long-standing argument. 'You see?'

And she beamed proudly at her knowledge-seeking son.

'He's looking at the windows,' murmured Constable Adams.

'I checked them,' replied Constable Downing, not sure whether to be affronted or worried. 'First thing I did yesterday. Told him so too.'

'Well, he's doing it again.'

Colonel Radcliffe was indeed re-examining the windows. In particular, those at the back of the building. He peered at them all closely. None of them showed any sign whatsoever of having been prised open.

Featherstone might conceivably have let in the murderer at the front door. But that door had been found locked and bolted. So Featherstone, or the murderer, must have locked and bolted it again from the inside. The murderer, then, must have left by a different route. The bolts on the small back door were welded in place by rust and had not been moved in years. That only left the windows. It had to be a window.

In a small storeroom on the first floor, Colonel Radcliffe finally found what he was looking for. Minute examination of the brass window catch revealed equally minute scratch marks.

'Downing,' he called.

'Yes, sir.'

'Take Adams with you and search the ground beneath this window.'

'We already have, sir.'

Colonel Radcliffe turned sharply. 'Then do it a second time. With your noses and fingertips, if necessary.'

'Yes, sir. Sorry, sir. Are we looking for something in particular?'

'A thread of wire.'

Colonel Radcliffe turned to the window again and smiled to himself. Pleased, relieved even. Now he would turn his attention to Mrs Barlow.

Jack could hear Mr Jevons coughing. He didn't go and say hello, just climbed the rickety wooden stairs to the low flat roof.

It was the only safe place for a secret meeting that Jack had been able to think of. Safe because the building underneath the flat roof was derelict. All the buildings on this side of the lane were derelict: Redbarn Road was to be widened and the owners and occupants of the poorly built factories and tenements had long since been required to leave. Only Jevons in his sweep's yard was likely to discover Jack and his new friends here.

He listened to Jevons talking to his horse as he harnessed it to the cart. More coughing. A lot more. Perhaps the sweep was really ill. Jack felt a sudden confusion of guilt and anger. He should be helping him, not trying to solve a crime, however dreadful. He wanted to talk to his old master, tell him what was happening, but he couldn't: it would be even more of a burden on the sick man now. At least Jevons wouldn't be worrying about him. He would assume Jack was with his father. He couldn't know that Tony Tolchard had slammed out of the house at dawn without a word to his son about their supposed new life together, let alone about the murder.

Jack determinedly told himself he had little enough to complain about, not compared to poor Richard Featherstone. And he resisted the temptation to just drop on to the sweep's cart as it left the yard and pretend nothing at all had happened. But he was very relieved when April appeared. He wasn't alone after all.

'No Rupert?' she observed, mildly sarcastic.

'I don't suppose he knows his way around the streets very well,' said Jack.

The nearest clock chimed ten and they sat in silence for a while.

'Gran says thank you for the sovereign,' announced April. 'I never told her about you being sick and everything.'

Jack shrugged. She was being gracious. He didn't know what to say.

April sprang up, hearing footsteps before Jack did.

'Well,' said Rupert, emerging on to the roof and looking around. 'Here we are then.'

He was clutching the morning newspaper, having managed to smuggle it from the breakfast room. April thought he seemed rather full of himself. He spread the newspaper on the roof.

'A woman was seen in Nunwell Street,' he said. 'By a clerk in one of the offices across the road. The papers are saying her name's Freda Barlow.'

Jack studied the newsprint and shook his head. 'There's no gaslight in front of number seventeen. I don't see how anyone could clearly see a face, not looking from a window opposite.'

'I agree,' said Rupert. 'We can forget the woman. It's got to be Erskine and the scaffolder.'

'I didn't say that –'

'You heard two men talking in Erskine's room.'

'Through the chimney?' April was becoming

irritated by Rupert's manner. 'One of them could easily have been a woman. Jack didn't *see* them. Did you?' she demanded.

Jack shrugged. 'No.'

'Well,' said Rupert, suddenly defensive, 'what difference does it make if one of them *was* a woman?'

'A lot,' said April, 'if you're going to keep on about scaffolders.'

'Forget scaffolders then,' said Rupert airily. 'That still leaves Erskine. I've deduced,' he continued importantly, 'that neither the housekeeper nor the maid were in the house at the time you were in the chimney. Erskine had the place to himself.'

'How d'you know that?'

'Because they always go to the market on Tuesday mornings with our cook.'

'Still doesn't prove it was him in the room,' retorted April.

'Then we'll just have to see what we *can* prove, won't we,' said Rupert with a rather smug smile. 'I have an appointment with Erskine at lunchtime. To discuss art.'

The announcement had the desired effect. Jack and April both stared at him.

'And while I keep him talking, Jack can search his room. He might find all kinds of evidence.'

'Such as what?' asked April.

Jack thought for a moment. 'Well,' he said, nodding at Rupert, 'I suppose the rope, for a start.'

'Exactly!' Rupert turned to April. 'It won't be a job for three,' he said. 'Perhaps you could find out more about this woman Freda Barlow? Meet us back here this afternoon.'

April felt she was being fobbed off, but she didn't complain.

Colonel Radcliffe had decided against having Mrs Barlow brought to the police station. The fact that she hadn't voluntarily come forward was disturbing, if indeed she was the woman seen outside Featherstone's office. But it was more than possible that the witness was wrong. Mrs Barlow might be entirely innocent. She might not know she'd been blatantly named by certain of the morning papers.

However, as his carriage turned into the street where she lived, Radcliffe saw there was no hope at all of a quiet, discreet interview in her own home. The crowd outside her house was ten deep. Clearly, the press could scent blood and a large number of the public liked the smell of it too. Newsmen and onlookers turned eagerly as they recognized the Assistant Commissioner.

'Come to make an arrest, sir?'

'Is it true she threatened to kill Featherstone?'

'Does she deny visiting Nunwell Street?'

'Why has she not come forward if she didn't do it?'

'What was the murder weapon, sir?'

'How did she get out?'

Colonel Radcliffe ploughed through to the front door, looking neither left nor right; answering nothing.

To his surprise, the front door opened as he reached it. Mrs Barlow closed it again behind him as soon as he was inside.

'Colonel Radcliffe, ma'am. Assistant Commissioner of Police.'

'Yes. I have seen your photograph. That is why I let you in.'

Clearly, she had been crying. She led him through to the parlour and indicated a chair. She herself paced the room tensely.

'You will know why I'm here, ma'am?'

'Of course. Of course . . .'

Radcliffe paused before asking the question.

'Did you visit Henry Featherstone on the night he was murdered?'

'Yes.' There was no hesitation. She looked at him and nodded, eager to speak. Too eager? 'Yes, I did . . . He had said I should, but at first I was too proud and angry.' She sat down, turning away from Radcliffe. 'Then all I could think of was that I hadn't enough money to bury Edwin properly.' She rocked back and forth where she sat, fists clenched in her lap. 'And Henry Featherstone was so kind . . . In spite of everything I'd said about him, he was so kind . . .' She wept, tears streaming down her face.

'He gave you money?' Radcliffe's questions were gentle but insistent.

She nodded. 'He gave me money. Not just for the funeral, but for our immediate debts as well . . .'

'Might I ask how much?'

'Two hundred pounds in cash.'

'A great deal, ma'am.'

'He said I didn't need to tell anyone where the money had come from: that I should just let people think one of Edwin's investments had proved a success after all.'

'Were you aware of Featherstone locking the street door again when you left?'

She nodded. 'Yes, indeed. He spoke of it as his constant routine.'

'And you saw or heard nothing else untoward? No one else in or near the building?'

She shook her head. Colonel Radcliffe found it difficult to doubt her honesty. But perhaps it was just the grief that was genuine, not her version of events.

'Then I shall trouble you no further at the moment, ma'am. Just . . .'

As he stood up, he drew from his pocket a flat, lidded tin and a fold of thickish paper.

'I wonder if you would be so kind . . . This is a procedure not unknown in India, where I was until recently engaged, and which I hope now to pioneer in England.' He opened the tin. Inside was what appeared to be a pad of damp, greasy soot. 'It's a kind of ink, ma'am, though it will wash off, I assure you. And it provides a means of identification – or in your case, I'm sure, elimination. May I?'

He took her hand politely, gently, placed her fingertips on the pad and then rolled them on the paper. She stiffened and recoiled. He let go of her hand and nodded at the black marks she'd left behind.

'Fingerprints, ma'am,' he said with a reassuring smile. 'Everyone's are different.'

Behind him, beyond the lace inner curtains, the face of a small girl who had wriggled her way through the crowd was pressed against the window.

Rupert let Jack in at the side gate.

'You'd better not use their fire escape,' he said. 'I don't know if the doors are kept unlocked. Use the backstairs instead. Their housekeeper's in our kitchen gossiping with Elizabeth so there's only their maid, Joan, to get past. Give me two minutes.

She should answer the front door when I knock.'

Jack ran at the creeper-covered dividing wall and scrambled swiftly up and over into next door's garden. Then he crouched where he could see the basement kitchen, and waited.

He heard Rupert's knock, deliberately loud, at the front door, and saw the maid disappear from the kitchen to answer it. Jack ran to the kitchen door, nipped inside and stood a moment, getting his bearings. The layout of the house was, he guessed, a mirror image of the Shoreys'. The backstairs, the servants' stairs, had to be through the door in front of him. He found them and bounded up two at a time. At the top of the second flight, he paused and cautiously opened the door into the corridor. No one about. He ran along to what he was sure must be the artist's room and quietly turned the door handle. The door was locked.

For a moment Jack stood staring at the brass doorknob, angry that neither he nor Rupert had anticipated this. He turned to retrace his steps, then realized what he must do.

'Hello, I'm Rupert. Very good of you to spare the time, sir.'

In the Knights' hallway, Hugo Erskine shook the proffered hand and tried to look pleased.

'No trouble at all,' he said. 'Though I am rather busy.'

'Yes, of course. Where are you working at the moment, sir? I'd love to see.'

Erskine showed Rupert into the dining room. All the furniture had been removed, stepladders and planks were propped in one corner, and the floor was covered by a huge dust sheet. A stag, poised haughtily on a mountain top, stared down from the wall opposite the door. Rays of sunshine streamed through cloudy skies behind the beast and a thick pine forest was sprouting in the foreground.

'Gosh,' said Rupert, gazing at the very life-sized and life-like animal.

'The client's choice,' said Erskine with a slight shrug, absolving himself of blame.

Two floors above, Jack squeezed himself into the fireplace of the Knights' attic room and began to climb. He reached the main chimney space, hesitated for a moment, then lowered himself into another narrow and very sooty flue. The Knights weren't as punctilious as the Shoreys about having their chimneys regularly cleaned.

He emerged in the fireplace of a first-floor room and crouched, rubbing soot from his eyes and stifling the urge to cough up the black dust he'd breathed into his lungs. His knees and elbows were scraped and bleeding a little but he was in the right room, the artist's room. The room in which he had heard murder plotted.

Jack stood up, wiping his hands on his shirt in an effort to clean them a little, and glanced quickly around. Everywhere there were paintings, some finished, some half finished, some on easels, some propped against the walls and the furniture. The bare floorboards were spattered with paint, and strips of canvas with daubs of different colours hung like washing on a line by the window. Cautiously, trying not to shed too much soot, Jack stepped away from the hearth, intending to search behind the canvases propped on the floor.

The painted faces seemed to look up at him as he hovered over them. A street singer, his mouth wide open, held out a cloth cap for pennies; a carpenter sawed a plank of wood; bricklayers sweated under hods full of bricks; and a group of scaffolders sat nonchalantly eating their lunch on a girder above a tumbling river. Jack was mesmerized. He'd never seen paintings before, not close up, not like this. He felt he wanted to speak to these people, to put a penny in the singer's cap and to balance on the girder with the scaffolders. He told himself off. *Concentrate.*

He skirted the room, peeping behind the canvases without actually touching them, but that was enough to see there were no coils of rope, no piles of sovereigns or bank notes. The furniture in the room consisted of a couple of battered old armchairs and an equally old kitchen table with one drawer. Jack wiped his hands on his shirt again before opening the drawer. It was stuffed full of scraps of paper, pencils, brushes, charcoal, palette knives, all the tools, he presumed, of the artist's trade.

Near the back of the drawer, he found a manilla envelope. It contained more scraps of paper: handwritten notes, lists and bills, but no money. Still, it was more interesting than anything else he'd found. Jack hesitated. He was no thief but perhaps, just perhaps, this could be useful. He slipped the envelope inside his shirt and shut the drawer. He could always get it back to the artist later. Somehow. He scanned the room again. He had to be quick now. There was no telling how long Rupert could keep Erskine talking.

Rupert was still in the half-painted dining room. Just. He'd exhausted his store of questions regarding the influence of classical art on the modern and was becoming desperate.

'So tell me, please,' he begged, 'about brushes.'

'Brushes?' repeated the long-suffering Erskine without enthusiasm.

'Yes, would you recommend squirrel hair or

badger? Or is there really nothing to match Siberian mink?'

'For oils or watercolour?'

'Uh, yes. Indeed. Both. Either. Of course.'

As Jack turned from the table in Erskine's room, he noticed again the scraps of canvas on their washing line by the window. Each one had splodges of paint, different colours daubed on singly then swirled together. He guessed the artist used these to experiment with mixing the shades he wanted for his canvases. One scrap in particular attracted his eye. The reds and blues and blacks were mixed in the centre to a deep bruise purple. But it wasn't the colour that had made him look more closely. In the barely dry paint, he could clearly see marks where the artist had held the canvas. Marks made by fingers. What had he heard about such marks? Quite recently. He couldn't remember but he reached up anyway and quickly unpegged the scrap of canvas, slipping it inside his shirt, next to the manilla envelope. Then he hurried back to the fireplace, scuffing his feet from side to side to obliterate the footprints he had made. Crouching beneath the mantelpiece, he blew some more damp, black dust from the hearth into the room, hoping to make it look as if there had been a sudden heavy fall of soot from an unswept chimney. With a bit of luck, Mr Jevons might even get another job.

Jack squirmed and clawed his way slowly up inside the flue until he reached the main chimney space again. There he paused, his feet braced against one wall, his back against the other, and silently spat soot from his mouth and rested his aching arms for a moment. He was anxious now about emerging back into the Knights' attic. Their maid or housekeeper could be anywhere now; quite possibly on the backstairs. If he tried to go out that way, he might be seen, stopped. He concentrated hard, trying to work out which flue would lead down into the Shoreys' attic instead. That would be a safer exit route. A sudden noise startled him, a key in a lock and footsteps on the bare boards below.

'Feather-brained child . . .' muttered Erskine.

He stopped in the middle of his room. Something was not quite right. He was used to remembering, visualizing the arrangement of objects. There was a gap in his line of colour samples. One was missing. It must have fallen from its peg into the litter beneath. No matter. He could find it later. And there must have been a fall of soot too. How messy. Everything was irritating but he was late, thanks to the idiot Rupert. He gathered up sketch pad and charcoal and hurried out.

Jack waited until he heard the key turning in the lock again, then eased himself down into the Shoreys' attic chimney. The room almost felt homely, he had been there so many times now. He hurried out into the passage, heading for the fire escape, then stopped. Someone was banging about in Rupert's room below. He crept to the top of the staircase and peeped down. Perhaps Rupert was back already. Softly, he descended a few steps so he could see through the open bedroom door. But it wasn't Rupert clattering about. It was Elizabeth, the maid. Her broom was propped against the chair, and clothes, boots and books she'd picked from the floor were piled on the bed. She was now on her hands and knees, pulling a black, grimy sack from underneath it. Jack retreated quickly as she straightened up. She was muttering crossly.

The returning Rupert met her downstairs at the kitchen door.

'Master Rupert! That filthy object in your room.'

Rupert swallowed hard.

'Look at my hands,' demanded Elizabeth, showing him her slightly blackened palms. 'I look like a sweep. I'm not touching it again.' She glared at him. 'Does your mother know about it?'

'Sorry, Elizabeth.' Rupert didn't answer her question. 'Very sorry. No need to mention it to

Ma, though. I'll get rid of it. And, um, don't worry about doing the rest of my room. I'll do that too.' He gave her a beseeching smile and hurried up the backstairs.

Safe in his room, the door closed behind him, Rupert peered under his bed. The sack with its grapnel had disappeared.

The pleasure of Tony Tolchard's company was wearing thin in the Cap and Cockerel. For one thing, he was now cadging drinks rather than standing them all round. The sovereigns were all spent, and he'd mislaid the card that Richard Featherstone had given him, so he had no money. Also, although he'd stopped boasting about his son, he'd become particularly derisive about the murder investigation. Evie and the other regulars were used to his superior knowledge on every subject so did their best to ignore him.

'No access,' he scoffed. 'No access? Course there was access. Has to be for a murder. Police don't know anything, Evie. Never did and never will.'

'Should consult you again then, shouldn't they, Tony? You'd put them right.' It was always best to humour him when he was drunk.

'Many a true word, my girl. Many a true word . . .'

Tony leant across the bar as if to impart a secret, then winked and tapped his nose and straightened up again. He steadied himself, located the pub door and wavered out into the daylight.

Evie and the regulars shook their heads and chuckled. None of them was aware of another drinker putting down his glass and slipping quietly out through the same door.

6

Father and Son

When he returned to the flat roof later that afternoon, Rupert was relieved to see that Jack had the grapnel.

'I had to come back into your attic,' explained Jack. 'Erskine's door was locked so I used the chimney. Then I saw your maid pull the grapnel from under your bed.' He grinned. 'Wasn't she cross. She marched off in a right old temper and as soon as she'd gone I nipped in and took it.'

'Excellent,' said Rupert. 'I was really worried.'

'We can't hide it in your room again,' said Jack. 'I'd better take it home with me.'

'That would be really stupid,' snorted April.

Both boys looked at her in surprise.

'Why?' asked Jack, a bit annoyed at being called stupid.

'Because you don't know for certain no one saw you on the roof at Nunwell Street. What if you were seen and the police traced you and came round to your place? If they find that under your bed, you'll be number one suspect. For murder.'

Jack looked at her but knew she was right.

'Where can we hide it then?' he asked, his voice betraying his fear and frustration.

April took the sack. 'I'll look after it,' she said. 'I know a few good hiding places.'

She smiled an enigmatic, slightly triumphant smile. Jack and Rupert glanced at each other and shrugged acceptance.

'Shall I tell you how I got on with Mrs Barlow?' asked April briskly, as if she were suddenly in charge.

'Uh, yes, please,' said Rupert. 'Did you find out anything?'

'There were a lot of people,' said April. 'The police moved them away in the end. There's a crusher outside her door now. Someone important came in a carriage. When I looked through the house window, he was pushing her hand in some soot. Then he wiped it off again on a piece of paper.'

Rupert was perplexed. 'Soot?'

April shrugged. 'Looked like it to me.'

'Oh,' said Rupert. 'I see.' He turned his attention to Jack instead.

'Any luck in Erskine's room?'

Jack shook his head. 'Not much. There wasn't any rope or money. All I found was this.'

He produced the envelope and the strip of canvas.

Rupert looked from one to the other then took the envelope and shook its contents out on to his lap.

'Well,' he said, regarding the bills and receipts and scraps of paper, 'if this is all we've got, we'd better have a look. Let's do a pile each.'

He started dividing the heap. April stood up and turned away. Rupert looked up, surprised, then noticed Jack mouthing silently at him behind her back.

'What?' mouthed back Rupert.

'She can't read,' said Jack without a sound.

'Oh.' Rupert hesitated. 'Er, I'll tell you what. Is anyone else hungry? I missed lunch.'

April always missed lunch. Rupert took a shilling from his pocket.

'What if April finds a cake seller or pastry man and fetches us something back, while we do the boring stuff?'

April took the shilling without a word, picked up the grapnel sack and was gone.

The handsprings were good. Erskine was fascinated by the tumblers' strength and agility as they somersaulted on to and off each other's shoulders.

He felt a warm glow here in the market, where

everything seemed bustle and good humour. Building sites lacked that. They made up for it in other ways, and those who worked on them were equally to be admired: they were the muscle and sinew of the nation. But markets, with their costermongers and street entertainers, their colour and vitality, were its beating heart.

Erskine settled down to sketch, eager not only to capture the scene in lines of charcoal, but also to be part of it. To belong. To this end, he threw aside his extravagant wide-brimmed hat and long swirling coat, and sat in his shirt sleeves like a common workman.

'You'll catch your death, Hugo,' remarked the man who had just arrived to sit beside him, clearly with no intention of removing his own coat and hat.

Erskine turned, surprised.

'Didn't expect to see *you* here today,' he said.

Colonel Radcliffe climbed swiftly into his carriage. He was vexed. The rank and file of E Division might regard an Assistant Commissioner with awe and jump to it when he gave an order, but he was not a law unto himself. He too had superiors. And when the Commissioner of Police himself summoned this new man from India to give an account of the case so far, he had no choice but to go. Everything else must wait.

Constables Adams and Downing had failed to find any threads of wire beneath the Nunwell Street back window and Radcliffe didn't doubt they had searched with their fingertips as instructed. But that didn't mean his theory was wrong. The scratches on the locking mechanism were real enough. There was so much still to do and here he was sitting in his carriage in a traffic jam. It could take an hour to get to Whitehall. Another hour back. Half a day wasted. He drummed his fingers in frustration.

April had been gone a long while. When she returned, without the grapnel, she handed three greasy pies and twopence change to Rupert. He put the money in his pocket and eagerly started munching. He wasn't allowed greasy pies at home.

Jack didn't comment on the change. Pies were a penny each, so seven pence had gone missing; probably, he suspected, in the form of lunch and dinner for April's gran. Rupert hadn't noticed and didn't need to worry about the true cost of pies. Jack gave April a look, to let her know he was aware. And left it at that. She looked back at him defiantly as she ate.

Rupert nodded at the scattered bits of paper in front of them.

'No luck,' he told April gloomily. 'No clues at

ll. Erskine's certainly not poor. He sells a lot of paintings. And buys an awful lot of paint.'

The word reminded Jack of the scrap of canvas he'd taken from Erskine's room. He delved under the bills and receipts and picked it up. Staring at it, he tried again to recall where the impulse to take it had come from. Then, quite suddenly, it began to come to him.

'Did you say the man who visited Mrs Barlow pushed her hand in some soot?' he asked excitedly.

April nodded, her mouth full.

'And then wiped it off again?'

April spat out a piece of gristle. 'Sort of.' She mimed the action, splaying her fingers and pressing them on the flat roof.

'What did he do with the paper?'

'Don't know. A crusher pulled me away from the window.'

Jack nodded and smiled. 'Fingerprints,' he announced. 'It's called fingerprints.'

He remembered now. It was one of the gems of information Mr Jevons had read aloud from a newspaper. 'Mr Jevons joked about it: said you couldn't be a sweep *and* a burglar because you'd always be getting caught.'

'Why?' asked April.

'Because of our sooty fingerprints. Everything we touched would have our marks on it. Because everyone's fingerprints are different. I'm sure that's what it said in his newspaper.'

April grunted and finished her pie, dismissive of newspapers which she couldn't read.

Jack quickly gathered the bits of paper back into their envelope and got to his feet.

'Come on. Mr Jevons is at work but Mrs Jevons won't mind us looking at the newspaper store.'

She didn't mind. On seeing Jack, she was pleased and concerned in equal measure, and confused by his new friends, especially Rupert. She didn't press too hard on exactly what Jack was looking for in the newspapers, but she did ask other awkward questions.

'Shouldn't you be at work, Jack? Hasn't your father found you something yet?'

'You're not to worry about me, Mrs Jevons. I'll be fine.'

And at that moment he felt fine: concerned for Mr Jevons, concerned for his father and responsible for solving the murder, but they were getting somewhere. He led the way through to the newspaper store, a mouldering pile of newsprint stacked in a shed in the backyard.

'It wasn't that long ago,' said Jack. 'Back in the spring, I think.'

He unloaded newspapers from the stack, and after several false starts, found the one he was looking for. He spread it on the ground and opened it.

'There.' He pointed at a headline, 'News From The Empire', and ran his fingers down the columns before pointing again and reading aloud, carefully and self-consciously.

'Readers will be interested to learn of a most curious means of identification which, it is understood, has been successfully used in India for many years. Workers and prisoners who are unable to write their names, are required to make an impression with their thumbs as an alternative to a personal signature. It has been shown that no two persons have the same thumbprints. Thumbs are used for the purpose, being the largest of the human digits, but the same principle applies to all fingers. The minute ridges and rings on a person's finger ends, when closely observed, are unique, and are not hered . . . heredit . . .'

'Hereditary?' offered Rupert. 'Not passed down from parent to child.'

Jack nodded. 'Hereditary.'

'And I've read about it too!' exclaimed Rupert.

April wasn't surprised.

'Well, not exactly – but the same idea. Pa's got a book on the Ancients: the Mesopotamians and Babylonians and suchlike, you know?'

They didn't.

'Well, the potters who made the vases and bowls and things in those days put a finger mark on the clay while it was still soft. Obviously as a kind of signature.'

Obviously, thought April. She stared at her finger ends. They looked no different from anyone else's. Jack went out of the shed and scooped a handful of damp soot from a bucket and spread it on a piece of wood, smoothing it to a thin paste.

'April,' he called. 'Come and do what Mrs Barlow did.'

Warily, April allowed Jack to press her fingertips on to the soot, then plant them on the envelope he'd taken from the artist's room. It was the only thing he had. April lifted her hand. The marks she left behind seemed nothing special. Jack repeated the process with his own fingertips.

'Look closely,' he said. 'Perhaps you'll see the difference.'

He wished they had Rupert's magnifying glass. That would make it clear. April nodded but she wasn't certain. Jack was, though. He held the scrap of painted canvas in front of April.

'See these marks here? They're fingerprints too, aren't they? And they're bound to be Erskine's. If we found the same marks at Featherstone's office, we'd know for certain that Erskine had been there.'

'Featherstone's office?' echoed Rupert. 'But it's locked and guarded. We could get life imprisonment for burglary.'

He looked at April, who shrugged. There was a brief silence. Rupert swallowed.

'When?' he asked quietly. 'Now?'

Jack shook his head. 'It's too light.'

'I have to be home before five,' said Rupert, slightly embarrassed, 'or else Ma will keep me in for a week. I could sneak out tonight, though, after dark.'

Jack shook his head again. 'We can't manage in pitch black either.'

'When, then?' asked April.

Jack shrugged. 'Tomorrow? Before dawn? I'll meet you both in the road next to Nunwell Street. You can keep watch for me.'

'All right,' said Rupert after another pause. He picked up Erskine's envelope of bills and receipts. 'And, um, I'll have another look at these, shall I?'

Jack nodded. 'Don't worry if you can't be there tomorrow.'

'I'll be there,' said Rupert.

They said goodbye and thank you to Mrs Jevons, and Rupert hurried away as the clock chimed five. Just for a moment, Jack wished fervently that he also had a mother who worried about where he was and what he was doing to go home to at the end of the day.

'How have you managed to keep all this from your pa?' asked April suddenly.

'He's never home,' said Jack.

He put the scrap of canvas back inside his shirt. 'I'll see you tomorrow.'

'Yes,' said April.

As she turned away, Jack was struck by a thought. 'Where did you hide the grapnel?'

'In a sewer, of course.'

'The Commissioner,' announced Colonel Radcliffe, 'asks me to convey to you all his satisfaction with your efforts so far, and his confidence that those efforts will bring this investigation to a speedy conclusion.'

The assembled ranks of E Division seemed pleased to have been praised by the Commissioner himself. Colonel Radcliffe did not confide in them the full extent of his conversation at Whitehall. Inwardly, he was seething because he had been made to feel foolish. The Commissioner had asked him, almost casually, the exact circumstances of the discovery of Featherstone's body. How many police officers had been present? Had one stayed at the door while the other, or others, went into the office? For if one had not stayed at the door, and the murderer had still been inside the building, was it not possible that the murderer had merely slipped out while the officers' backs were turned? Merely slipped out. It had been suggested with a shrug. But, of course, it was possible. It was basic.

And Colonel Radcliffe, who prided himself on overlooking nothing, indeed had been appointed for that very reason, had overlooked it.

'Constable Adams,' he called before dismissing the rest of the men. 'Please come to my office.'

Adams felt his blood drain into his boots. He trudged after the Assistant Commissioner while his colleagues stared at him before melting away.

In the office, Colonel Radcliffe turned straight to him.

'I want you to tell me exactly, *exactly* what happened when you arrived at Featherstone's office on the day his body was found. Who was with you – apart from the son?'

'Constable Willis, sir.'

'It was just the two of you?'

'Yes, sir. Just me and Willis.'

The Colonel had begun pacing in a circle around him. It made Adams feel giddy.

'Willis broke in, yes?'

'He did, sir. Unlocked and unbolted the door. Let in myself and Richard Featherstone.'

'Who went into the actual office first?'

'Richard Featherstone, sir. We followed him in.'

'Both of you.'

'Both of us, sir. The father's body was on the floor. The son was very upset, of course. So we pulled him away – we took an arm each and pulled him out of the office. Then we went back in to examine the body.'

'Both of you?'

'Both of us, sir.'

Colonel Radcliffe spoke with cool precision. 'So there was a moment of time when neither you nor Willis was watching the street door?'

Oh dear, thought Adams. *Oh dear, oh dear. This is what it's about.*

'Is that correct, Adams?'

'Yes, sir. That's correct. Only for a few seconds. We didn't think −'

'No,' said Colonel Radcliffe. 'You didn't.'

'I'm sorry, sir.'

'We all make mistakes, Adams. In the heat of the moment.' Colonel Radcliffe found himself being magnanimous. He had no right to be otherwise. 'It's important that we acknowledge and learn from them.'

'Yes, sir.'

Adams blinked. That appeared to be all. He hadn't been sacked. Perhaps he should chance mentioning the prophetic sweep's boy. But the Colonel's stare was still harsh.

'Anything else?'

Adams shook his head. 'No, sir.'

One acknowledged mistake at a time was enough.

*

Jack was also screwing up his courage. The window. He had to know about the window. He couldn't put it off any longer. He'd taken the long route home, rehearsing what he would say to his father, the questions he would ask and how he would ask them. It was almost dark when he finally reached the street door and went in.

As he climbed the stairs, he could hear voices. They became raised and there was the noise of a chair scraped back and falling over. Jack thought it must be the neighbours arguing again. Then he recognized one of the voices as his father's.

'I've said nothing. Nothing.'

'That's not what I've heard. You talk too much. And there's only one way to stop that.'

Another scrape of furniture followed the threat. Jack threw open the door and burst into the room. In the shadowy gloom he saw his father helpless on his back, sprawled across the table with another man's hands tightly round his neck. Jack could hear the panicked gurgling gasps. His father was being choked to death.

Jack rushed at the assailant and tried to pull him off. The man reacted violently. Letting go of Tony, he lunged and grabbed at Jack instead.

Jack ducked the powerful hands and butted the man in the stomach. As the man staggered backwards, Jack clung on to him, head down, butting again and again at the hard muscular belly. Tony had scrambled away now and was standing, his back to the wall, gulping in air, watching as his assailant and Jack crashed into the table. For a moment it looked as if Jack, now on top of the other man, would get the better of him, but then the table capsized under the sudden new weight. The noise as it toppled over, followed by the desperately struggling man and boy, provoked hammering on the wall from the people next door.

Tony danced around ineffectually but did nothing to help as the stronger man wrenched his arm free and, grabbing Jack by the hair, jerked his head back painfully. Jack yelled, tried to roll away, and man and boy, still locked together, thudded against the wall. The banging from the neighbours changed instantly to angry threats to call the police. The man paused for a second, listening to the shouts from the next room, then he shoved Jack hard in the chest, forcing him away. For the first time, Jack got a good look at his face.

It wasn't Erskine. It wasn't the scaffolder. It was no one he recognized. The man aimed one more blow at Jack then fled, leaving the door open behind him.

A peculiar silence followed. No neighbour came to complain or see what the trouble was. The only sound Jack could hear was his own rapid breathing and the thumping of his heart.

His father said nothing. Didn't explain. Didn't thank him. Merely closed the door and began slowly to right the furniture.

'Who was he?' Jack finally managed to ask.

His father shrugged. 'No idea. A burglar, maybe.' He attempted a joke. 'Came to the wrong place here.'

'Will you stop lying to me!' Jack was trembling. 'Just stop lying to me!'

Tony turned and regarded him. 'Calm down, son,' he said, venturing another slight smile.

But Jack couldn't calm down. 'You were paid to leave a window open, weren't you?'

Tony frowned, deliberately blank. 'Window? What window?'

'Nunwell Street. Where you work. You left it open.'

'Left it open?'

'You left it open for the murderer!' shouted Jack.

It was out. The boil was burst. In the silence that followed, he stood glaring at his father, willing him not to lie again. He was still shaking and his fists were clenched.

His father merely looked at him as if he were a two-year-old.

'Don't be stupid, boy. All the windows were locked.'

Jack's arms dropped to his sides. He threw his

head back and closed his eyes for a moment.

'No,' he said through clenched teeth. 'One of them was left unlocked. It was locked after the murder. From the *outside*. Wasn't it?'

Again the attempted smile. 'Who's filled your head with this nonsense?'

'No one's filled my head. It's what happened. I can prove it.'

'What d'you mean, you can prove it?' The smile was suddenly gone. 'Are you in with the police?'

'No!'

'Then how d'you know so much?'

'It doesn't matter how I know. What matters is if it's true!'

Tony blew a long sigh, then shrugged.

'All right. I left the window open. In the storeroom at the back. It was a mistake. Not doing my job properly. Forgetful. Careless. That's all. I should have said. Told someone. But you know what it's like. If you don't tell the truth straight away, it gets more and more difficult . . .'

Jack was already shaking his head miserably.

'You're still lying! Lying . . . I just heard that man saying you talk too much. Why would he say that if it was just a mistake? If you just forgot! I'm your son. Two nights ago you told me I was a man now. If you're in trouble, I want to help you. But you have to tell me the truth!'

Tony turned away. He slowly sat down and

stared into the empty grate for a long time. At last he spoke, in a flat voice, not looking at Jack.

'Yes, I left it open on purpose.'

Jack said nothing. There was another silence.

'The man who was here . . . He came up to me in the pub. On the day . . . on the day it happened. At lunchtime. I go to the pub at lunchtime. I didn't know him. He said he'd followed me.' Tony paused. 'He offered me money to leave the back window open. A lot of money.' Tony looked up. 'I swear, Jack, I didn't know it was for murder. I wanted the money for you. So we could set up properly together. Have a future. Don't turn your back on me. Please!'

But Jack had to look away. He stared at the door, thinking of the Cap and Cockerel and the pile of sovereigns on the bar. Behind him, his father's voice gradually became a whine.

'They've cheated me, Jack. Drawn me in, used me, and now they want me dead. The one who was here, he's not working on his own, I'm sure of it. I'm a marked man, Jack. And if they don't get me, the police will. There'll be no mercy. If they find out about the window, I'll hang. You don't want your father to hang, do you? Son? Do you?'

'A man is dead because of what you did for money.' Jack's voice was high and thick. He choked back tears.

'No, Jack, no. I've told you. I never knew it was for murder. I was tricked. I'm as innocent as Featherstone himself!' Tony sprang up from the chair, suddenly all restless energy. 'Look, boy, look. I have to leave here and you must come too. We'll start again, eh? Put this all behind us. Go north where no one knows us. There's work there, in the cities. Money to be made, lots of it. Maybe even start our own business. You and me together.' He put his hand on Jack's arm. 'Father and son.'

Jack flung out his arm, shaking his father off. Tony raised his fist and for a split second seemed about to strike the boy. Then he lowered it again.

'You're not a man,' he sniffed. 'You're just a boy.' His voice rose higher. 'Well, stay here then. I don't care. Just promise you won't betray me. Eh? Promise me!'

Jack couldn't speak. He could hardly breathe. He pressed his face into the wall.

'Damn you to hell then!' screamed his father.

The wall shook against Jack's wet face as the door slammed beside him.

7

Connections

Jack woke with the daylight. He'd cried himself to sleep and his eyes felt crusted with salt. He raised himself on an elbow and looked towards the bed. It was empty. His father hadn't come back. He flopped down again and stared at the ceiling. He wanted nothing but to curl up in a tight ball of misery. That was how he'd spent the night, trying to shut everything out. But nothing really changed when you did that. Nothing went away.

He became aware of voices, down at the street door, then footsteps on the stairs. He sprang up from his blanket on the floor. The police? Had his father already been arrested? Or killed?

There was a tap at the door.

'Who's there?'

'Jack? Is that you?' Rupert's voice was cautious.

Jack suddenly remembered where he was supposed to have been before dawn. He opened the door. April was there with Rupert. She looked warily in past Jack.

'You on your own?' she asked quietly.

Jack nodded.

April looked at him. 'What's the matter?'

Jack turned away and sat down on the chair by the fireplace. April and Rupert glanced at each other and followed him into the room. Rupert closed the door.

'We, uh, went to Nunwell Street,' he said. 'Did you forget?' He could sense more than forgetfulness but didn't know what else to ask.

Finally, Jack spoke without looking up.

'When I came home yesterday, a man was trying to kill my father. He was being strangled on that table.'

Rupert started slightly and moved away from it. He regarded the shabby, ordinary piece of furniture and felt an unpleasant cold tingle. The reality of murder truly struck him for the first time.

'The man ran away,' said Jack. 'And my father's gone too.' He looked up at April. 'I told you he was a caretaker. I didn't tell you where. He worked for Henry Featherstone at Nunwell Street. And he was paid money to leave the window open. It was him. He admitted it to me last night.'

'Gosh . . .' said Rupert. 'I'm sorry, Jack. How awful for you.'

There was a silence before April spoke.

'So . . . who was it tried to kill him?' she asked.

'I don't know. I think whoever paid my father has decided he's a risk. He talks too much when he's drunk.' There was an empty bitterness in the last remark. 'And drunk or sober, he lies all the time. Boasts one minute, denies everything the next.' Jack sighed. 'I'm really not sure if he knew why they wanted the window left open or not. But it makes no difference. If he's caught, he'll hang.'

April crouched in front of Jack.

'Never mind your pa for a minute,' she said. 'You can't stay here, Jack. The man who came after your father might come back. And now you've seen him, he'll certainly want to kill you as well.'

Jack slowly looked up at her. April didn't blink.

'You have to leave, Jack. Now. It's not safe here.'

The three of them walked south, towards the river.

After a while, Rupert spoke.

'Would you like me to follow Erskine again? Find out more about the scaffolder? We don't want to get your pa in trouble but we don't want him murdered either.'

'There's no point,' said Jack. 'It wasn't either of them who attacked my father.'

Rupert fell silent again. Jack suddenly stopped walking.

'I think I'd like to be on my own for a bit,' he said, and turned away.

Rupert made to follow but April stopped him.

'Let him be,' she said. But she called after Jack fiercely. 'Don't go home. Right?' Then more gently: 'And meet us at Rupert's house this evening.'

Jack made no response.

Colonel Radcliffe carefully unfolded the piece of paper. Mrs Barlow's fingerprints were still intact and unsmudged. He laid the paper on his desk and placed the bloodstained chair leg from Featherstone's office next to it. The fingerprint in the blood wasn't very clear, but clear enough. He examined it again closely, through his magnifying glass, and compared it to Mrs Barlow's. But no matter how long he pored over the prints he couldn't convince himself that there was a match. In fact, he was convinced that there wasn't.

He turned to the constables gathered uncomfortably in his office.

'Gentlemen. I would like a second opinion.'

Without waiting for a volunteer, he handed the magnifying glass to Constable Adams and indicated for him to take a look. 'Take your time.'

Adams took the glass. *Why me?* he asked himself. He'd never held a magnifying glass before, and when he first peered through it, he started back a little: the bloody chair leg seemed to leap up at his face. He heard a couple of his colleagues stifle laughter.

'What do you see, Adams?' asked Colonel Radcliffe.

'Lots of little lines, sir. Sort of loops and swirls.' This sounded silly. Adams became convinced he'd been picked out to be made a fool of.

'Do any of the patterns on the paper match the single pattern on the chair leg?'

Adams moved the glass above the paper then back to the chair leg, studying both. He thought the correct answer was probably yes, but the loops and swirls didn't match. When you looked hard they were quite different, or seemed so to him. He looked up helplessly.

'Not that I can see, sir. Sorry, sir.'

'Which almost certainly means,' announced Colonel Radcliffe, glad to have his own observations confirmed, 'that Mrs Barlow did not kill Featherstone.'

Adams was relieved. He had some sympathy for Mrs Barlow. He was even more relieved when Colonel Radcliffe took back the magnifying glass.

The Assistant Commissioner continued briskly.

'The chair leg fingerprint does not belong to Mrs Barlow and it does not belong to Featherstone himself – I have been to the mortuary to compare it; so we must spread our net a little wider.'

His thoughts had already returned to the window with the scratched locking bar. 'Tell me: who are the best burglars that you know? If we were looking for a villain who is agile, who can climb like a cat, like a spider, who would you name?'

Adams flinched then stared at his feet. Colonel Radcliffe noticed and, while the others came out with the names of known cat burglars and safe breakers, he was only half listening.

'Yes, Adams?' he enquired.

Adams started and looked up guiltily. He had to come out with it this time. 'Well, it's nothing to do with burglars, sir, but there's something else I perhaps should have reported before . . .' He shrugged haplessly. 'But at the time it didn't seem . . .'

'Say what you have to say, man.'

'Yes, sir.' Adams straightened up, trying to ignore the fact that all eyes in the room were on him. 'On the afternoon of the murder I was approached on my beat by a sweep's boy. He told me there was going to be a murder that night in Nunwell Street. He didn't know what number, because, he said, the information had come to him in a dream.'

There was an ominous silence. Adams gulped and looked straight ahead.

'A sweep's boy?'

'Yes, sir.'

'Did you take his name?'

'No, sir. I just sent him on his way. At the time I assumed he was hoaxing me.'

It must be the sack now, thought Adams. *It must.* But the explosion didn't happen.

'Well,' said Colonel Radcliffe after a few seconds, 'sweeps' boys can certainly climb. Do we have anything else on sweeps or their boys?'

The question was met with a uniform shaking of heads. Then Constable Downing suddenly snapped to attention and raised his arm.

'Sir!' he said excitedly. 'The caretaker. Tolchard. His boy's a sweep.'

He was pleased with the effect of this revelation on those around him.

'He is?' The Assistant Commissioner tried to recall the boy he'd seen in Tony Tolchard's room. 'The one we saw? He wasn't dressed like a sweep.'

Downing nodded. 'But he is, sir. When I picked him up drunk, he gave his name and address honestly enough. And his occupation as sweep's boy. It's in the station log.'

A murmur of excitement rippled round the room. Hadn't they said all along that Tolchard was the most likely suspect? A caretaker who may have failed to lock windows now proved to have a son who could climb like a cat. Simple.

Only Adams seemed troubled. Colonel Radcliffe allowed him to ask the question.

'But surely, sir, the lad who spoke to me can't have been Tolchard's boy. I mean, if he was involved, why would he try to warn us?'

'Only one way to find out, mate.' Downing grinned, then remembered himself and snapped smartly back into rank. 'Sorry, sir.'

Colonel Radcliffe regarded Downing coolly, then nodded and addressed the room.

'Arrest Tony Tolchard,' he ordered. 'And his son.'

The constables filed eagerly out. Adams kept his head down but didn't escape unnoticed.

'Thank you, Adams,' said the Colonel mildly. 'We'll make a policeman of you yet.'

Out in the public office, the constables' excitement at their new task was overheard by Richard Featherstone as he arrived at the station. Seeing Colonel Radcliffe, he headed straight for him.

'There's a development?' he asked.

'Of a kind, sir. We need to speak again to your father's caretaker and to the man's son, who it seems may have had pre-knowledge of the crime.'

Richard frowned. 'Pre-knowledge?'

'Yes, sir. A sweep's boy spoke to one of my men before the event. Tolchard's son is a sweep's boy.'

'I see. And on that basis they are guilty?'

'I didn't say that.'

'You imply it.'

'No, sir. But they must be questioned further.'

Richard indicated the policemen behind him. 'So your pack is set to hounding them. Why do you not pursue your other suspects in such numbers?'

'We have no other suspects,' replied Colonel Radcliffe candidly.

'Then it would appear to be as I've protested all along: the working class are blamed for everything.'

'No, sir. I shall question them as fairly as I would your good self.'

'Take care you do, Colonel,' warned Richard. 'Or I shall take steps to have you removed from this case.'

Jack was sitting alone on the flat roof behind Jevons' yard. The cart wasn't there but he could hear Mrs Jevons doing the washing, her young children playing around her. Jack had kept himself out of their sight. Mrs Jevons would be kind and sympathetic and her kindness would be too much to bear. He didn't want to cry again. He sat chewing his lip, going over and over the conversation with his father and desperately trying to decide what he should do next. Suddenly, he heard footsteps and the creaking open of the yard gate.

'Are you there, missus? Police.'

Jack flattened himself on the roof. Why were they here?

'We knocked at the front door,' said the policeman. 'Can we come in?'

Mrs Jevons had a quiet voice. Jack strained his ears.

'Yes. Of course. What do you want? Is my husband all right?'

'I wouldn't know, ma'am, but I hope so. We're looking for a boy. A sweep's boy, name of Jack Tolchard. D'you know him?'

Jack's heart began to beat very fast and his limbs tensed. He shifted slightly, ready to run.

'Jack? Yes. He used to work for us. A good boy. What's wrong?'

'Used to work for you?'

'Yes. He left us earlier this week.'

'Any idea where we might find him?'

'No, none at all. His father took him.'

'Not doubting your word, you understand, ma'am, but d'you mind if we have a look around?'

'No. No, of course. Do as you must.'

The policemen began searching the yard. Jack silently climbed from his hiding place and stole away.

It seemed he was safe nowhere.

8

Break-in

Rupert and April had walked across London Bridge and back across the new Westminster Bridge, virtually in silence. They felt awkward in each other's company.

'We're not helping Jack,' said Rupert, suddenly impatient. 'Let's do something useful. Let's have another look at the clues we've got.'

They found a quiet churchyard and April sat watchfully beside a gravestone while Rupert squatted down, emptied the bills and receipts from their envelope again and divided them into piles. These were different piles, Rupert assured her, but they looked much the same as before to April. One pile was becoming much bigger than the rest, though. And the same bold print appeared at the top of all the receipts on it.

'Paterson and Jenkins,' said Rupert, pointing at the headed paper. 'Paterson and Jenkins, Suppliers to the Arts. That means paint and stuff. I think we should pay them a visit.'

'What for?'

'Because this one . . .' Rupert plucked up a particular Paterson and Jenkins receipt and held it meaningfully towards April, '. . . is dated the ninth. Three days ago.'

April didn't immediately understand.

'The day of the murder,' said Rupert. 'The day Jack heard the voices in Erskine's room. Erskine was at the art shop the same day. Maybe, just maybe, the other voice Jack heard was with him. We could get a description!'

Jack had found himself a new hiding place of a kind: a roofless, burnt-out building where there appeared to have been a chimney fire. The rats retreated from the basement when he crept in, and left him in peace. He crouched, listening to people passing by on the pavement above; the different footsteps. There seemed to be a lot of policemen.

He slept a little and each time he awoke he felt swiftly inside his shirt to make sure the scrap of canvas was still there. He'd decided that all his hopes depended on it now. If he could find a fingerprint at Nunwell Street to match Erskine's, then he would have solved the crime. He could show the police and they would talk to the judges. Judges were often sympathetic to criminals who helped the courts. Surely a judge would be lenient to a man whose son had caught the murderer. Maybe his father would be given a prison sentence instead of being hanged.

Jack's eagerness to obtain his proof made him impatient for the day to pass, despite the danger ahead. If he were caught, then that would be the end of everything. Nobody would believe his story. But he would not get caught. He felt a slight pang of guilt because April and Rupert would be waiting for him at Calborn Gardens and he had decided to act alone. But he didn't change his mind. He touched the scrap of canvas for the hundredth time. No, he would not get caught.

The shop assistant smiled helpfully at Rupert and tried to ignore the unwashed little girl who appeared to be with him.

'Yes, young man?'

'I'm a friend of Hugo Erskine's,' announced Rupert.

'Oh, really?' The shop assistant beamed. 'A very nice gentleman and a splendid artist.'

'Yes, indeed. D'you by any chance remember him calling here three days ago? On Tuesday the ninth?'

He should remember, thought Rupert. *Erskine spent a lot of money on Siberian mink brushes.*

'And why would you want to know that?' The assistant was still smiling.

Rupert hadn't thought of a reason.

'Mr Erskine's lost his pocketbook,' said April behind him. 'This is the last shop he can remember having it in.'

'Oh dear,' said the assistant, and immediately set himself to think. 'Well, yes, he *was* here on Tuesday but I'm sure he had his pocketbook when he left. He certainly didn't leave it.'

'Did he have a friend with him?' asked Rupert.

The assistant frowned briefly. 'A friend?'

'Yes,' said Rupert eagerly. 'Can you describe him?'

The assistant looked at Rupert, a hint of suspicion on his face. 'No, I can't. Mr Erskine was perfectly alone as usual.'

The doorbell jangled and a new customer came in.

'If you'll excuse me . . .' said the assistant.

'Um . . . if you could possibly remember the exact time,' stumbled Rupert, 'it would help Mr Erskine a lot.'

Jack slipped easily through the market, merging with the crowd. Dusk was finally approaching. Soon the great flares would be lit, giving a glow of magic to the business of buying and selling and picking pockets. The street performers looked better at night too: their costumes less threadbare and tawdry; their tricks and skills more breathtaking.

Jack suddenly stopped. There ahead of him was Erskine himself, seated amongst a group of other artists. Erskine looked up and Jack drew hastily back into the shadows behind a market stall, cursing himself for being careless. Surely Erskine must have seen him; Jack was certain there'd been a reaction, if only slight. But Erskine calmly resumed mixing paint on his palette.

Eventually, Jack edged away behind the stalls and continued by a different route. He didn't see the short, muscular man detach himself from the group around the artists and begin to follow. Jack looked back frequently to make sure there was no one on his trail. Each time, his pursuer sensed the movement and slid out of sight.

When Jack reached Nunwell Street, he found only one policeman on duty, standing sentry outside the door of number seventeen. The face under the tall hat seemed vaguely familiar but Jack didn't recognize Constable Adams.

Adams hated sentry duty. Officially, protecting the crime scene was a very important job. Unofficially, it was eight hours of boredom and discomfort. The night stretched numbingly ahead. It wasn't even dark yet. He had decided he would walk up and down every fifteen minutes, to relieve the monotony. A church clock struck the quarter and he turned sharply away from his spot outside the front door, marching left along Nunwell Street. Behind him at the other end of the street, a slight figure flitted across towards the rear of the building.

Jack paused by the now familiar drainpipe, listening and watching, making sure he was alone; then climbed quickly, anxious that he'd waited too long and would end up groping around inside the building in the dark.

On the roof he stopped, calming himself. *Slow down. Take your time. Don't get careless.*

Suddenly, he thought he heard a sound below, at the foot of the drainpipe. He froze. Listened ... Nothing. He crept slowly back to the roof edge and peered over. There was nothing to see in the shadows below. Nothing to see and nothing to hear. *Calm down. Calm down. You'll fall.* Nerves were as dangerous as haste. He picked his way up to the first roof ridge and sat astride it for a moment, listening again. Still nothing. He slid silently down into the first roof valley, then up and over into the second. He heard no noise except an occasional cough from the lone policeman.

When he reached the valley above number seventeen, Jack found the broken and loose roof tiles as he'd left them. He lifted the tiles carefully aside, hesitated a moment, then dug his fingers into the rotten wood and fabric that lined the inside of the roof. When he'd made a hole, he peered down through it into the space beneath, a kind of attic or loft, with wooden joists and a lot of dust and cobwebs. He made the hole bigger and, without a backward glance, eased himself down through and into the building.

Balanced, cat-like on the roof ridge behind him, a figure watched until Jack had disappeared, then edged softly down into the valley after him.

It was hot and windowless in the roof space. And dark. Jack searched the floor with his hands and found the loft hatch, just a square wooden lid, and lifted it out. Light of a kind entered from below. There was no ladder. Jack squatted for a second on the edge of the hole, then swung himself down and dropped lightly on to the first-floor landing. He paused for a moment, visualizing exactly where on the roof he had found the grapnel and where the window below it was positioned. It should be behind the door to his right. Cautiously, he pushed the door open. And there it was. He was looking directly at a sash window. *The* sash window. It was shut now but it had to be the window his father had left unlocked, the window the murderer had climbed through.

Jack padded over to it. Yes, it had exactly the same type of locking bar as those in Rupert's house. He peered out briefly at the ground below.

It would have been easy enough to throw a grapnel from there to the gutter above. He glanced quickly around the room. It was an office store with cabinets and cupboards but nothing else. He suddenly felt reluctant to go further, to trace the steps of the murderer and actually see the place where it had happened. He took a deep breath and went out on to the landing again, then walked slowly down the staircase to the ground floor.

The street door was straight in front of him. Jack paused for a moment, listening to the policeman's cough. It sounded frighteningly close. Because of it, he didn't hear the brush of clothing against wood, the light sound of breathing as someone bigger than himself squirmed through the hole into the roof space high above.

The office door was open. Jack made himself go in. He recoiled slightly in the doorway, shocked by the amount of blood. It was dry now, soaked darkly into the wood of the floorboards, desk and skirting board. Could his father really have known this was going to happen?

Jack tried to concentrate on his task, his reason for coming. He thought he could see a fingerprint in the bloodstains on the skirting board. He took out the precious scrap of canvas from inside his shirt and crouched to look closer.

There definitely was a fingerprint on the skirting board, but when he held the canvas against it he found comparison impossible. He shifted his position, but there was so little light now he still couldn't see properly. He was on his hands and knees, his nose almost on the skirting board, trying desperately to compare the prints, when he heard the sound. Not outside, not the policeman coughing. Inside. On the stairs.

Jack held his breath. He remained perfectly motionless, hoping he'd imagined it. Then he heard it again: the lightest footstep and pause. After a few seconds, another. Someone was descending the stairs, very slowly, stealthily. Stopping and listening. Trying to locate him.

Jack glanced around the office. There was only the one doorway. Unless he moved now he would be cornered, trapped. He thought fleetingly of banging on the window, or running to the front door and calling to the policeman for help. That might save him but only if the policeman was very quick. He tried to envisage the back of the building. There were windows on the ground floor. He had to make for one of them. Still clutching his scrap of canvas, he slowly straightened up. Then, like a rabbit, he bolted.

As he flashed down the hallway towards the back of the building, Jack glimpsed a dark shape on the stairs. But only for a second. The figure vaulted the banister and landed in front of him with the grace and menace of a wild animal. Jack stifled a cry of terror and crashed blindly past. He hurtled through the nearest open doorway and slammed the door behind him. There was no key in the lock. He vaulted across a table in the middle of the room and shoved it hard back against the door and leant against it. He heard a voice outside, cursing.

The door strained and rattled as the man outside put his shoulder to it and pushed. Jack knew he wouldn't be able to hold the table for more than a few seconds. He turned desperately back into the room. It was a caretaker's store with buckets and mops and piles of cleaning rags. And a window: a small fixed pane set in the wall, with no means of opening it. Jack grabbed a bucket and crashed it against the sealed glass. It shattered noisily but as the cascade of glass hit the ground outside, he also heard the sound of the table scraping back and the door bursting open. His pursuer was in the room. Jack turned momentarily and stared into the face of the man who had tried to strangle his father.

The bucket was still in Jack's hand. He hurled it at the man, who ducked and threw up his arms as the bucket glanced off the side of his head before bouncing and clattering away.

In the few precious moments he had gained, Jack seized a handful of cleaning rags and dumped them on the jagged glass in the window frame, then dived headfirst through. He cried out as he felt the man's powerful fists close round his ankle, but kept dragging himself out, writhing and kicking with his free foot. Then he felt the man's grip suddenly loosen as his hands were pulled by Jack's weight across the slicing remains of glass.

Jack fell in a heap on hard ground. His arms were bleeding but there was nothing he could do about that. He could hear shouting and the vigorous clacking of a policeman's rattle. His assailant loomed in the gaping window space above him. Jack rolled away, got to his feet and ran.

Constable Adams had been about-turning at the far end of Nunwell Street when he'd heard the commotion. At first it didn't occur to him that it could be happening inside the very building he was supposed to be guarding. But as he paced rapidly back towards number seventeen and on past the front door, the possibility seized him and he raised the alarm, springing his rattle and shouting for assistance.

Racing round the corner towards the back, he collided heavily with something small and fast. A boy. A boy he vaguely recognized. Adams grabbed at his hand but it was slippery with blood and the boy wriggled free. There was someone else in the lane behind number seventeen as well, running off in the opposite direction.

'Take that one!' roared Adams to the two beat policemen who had answered his rattle, and he raced off in pursuit of Jack.

Constable Adams knew now who the boy was. The whiff of soot from his clothes had given him away. The prophetic sweep's boy. Had that been his father with him? Why were they here?

Adams' knees and lungs were beginning to hurt but he didn't slow down. This was the catch he wanted. This would redeem him fully. He did his best to keep the boy in sight, and when he lost him briefly, there was a trail of blood to follow.

Jack dodged down alleyways and clambered over walls but he couldn't shake the policeman off. And Jack's ankle was beginning to slow him. It was cut and twisted from his escape through the window. He wanted to climb, to get on to a roof, but he wasn't far enough ahead, never out of sight for long enough.

Then, abruptly, he was in a dead end and he panicked until he realized he was at the railway workings where he and Rupert had followed Erskine and seen the scaffolder.

Jack eased between the hoardings and stumbled, then rolled down the muddy slope. He lay panting for a moment, then the hoarding creaked as the policeman also squeezed through. The site was dark and empty. No workmen or artists. Only the huge bare skeleton of ironwork. Jack crawled towards it and then climbed until he reached the highest level, and there became part of the skeleton himself, lying with his body flat and thin along a narrow scaffold board.

Constable Adams picked his way across the mud and rubble of the site. He was sweating and breathing hard, and wasn't sure the boy had come this way. He struck a lucifer and lit his lantern. Its beam probed the ironwork but showed him nothing. Not even spots of blood.

'Come out, if you're here, boy,' he called as sternly as he could while out of breath.

Nothing moved.

Adams started to climb a ladder but his muddy boots slipped on the rungs and he fell back again, painfully. He hesitated, made a reluctant decision, and hobbled away.

'I don't think he's coming.'

It had been a bad day and Rupert feared the worst.

'We didn't say a time,' said April doggedly.

They stood on the fire escape in silence for a while longer, straining their eyes towards the garden wall, but no one climbed nimbly over it.

'Look,' said Rupert awkwardly. 'I'm going to have to go in. My pa will be home at any minute and he always does the locking up. Maybe you should go home to your gran.'

'Maybe.' April shrugged, still reluctant.

'We'll try the flat roof in the morning,' suggested Rupert. He paused. 'I'll bring some food.'

April eventually looked at him and nodded. 'All right.'

They crept down to the garden and Rupert let April out of the side gate. There was no point in doing otherwise but he felt guilty closing it behind her.

He'd almost made it to his room when he heard his father arrive in the hallway down below, just home from a business dinner.

'Traffic was solid,' Mr Shorey announced to his wife. 'Police everywhere. They're not saying much but there's been more goings-on at Nunwell Street.'

'Nunwell Street?'

'Featherstone's place. Apparently they're after a sweep's boy.'

'A sweep's boy? Whatever for, dear?'

'What for? Murder, of course. Whoever he is, they think he's in it up to his neck.'

Rupert shrank into his room.

9

The Painting

Seventeen Nunwell Street was now full of light. The gas lamps had all been lit and lanterns swayed and flashed in the darker corners of the building. Colonel Radcliffe was already there by the time Constable Adams limped back.

'It was definitely him, sir. Definitely the sweep's boy.'

Colonel Radcliffe was perplexed. Why on earth would the boy return to the scene of the crime? Except that it was commonly believed that murderers often did. In a macabre way it made more sense of the boy's initial approach to Adams, with talk of a dream. Perhaps he had known he was going to kill and wanted to be stopped. That was not unknown either. Colonel Radcliffe tried to shake off such fanciful ideas. He had seen the boy, and the father, three mornings ago. He was sure they were implicated in some way but far from sure they could have personally killed Featherstone.

'And no trace at all of the other man?'

He'd already asked Constable Downing the question once.

'Afraid not, sir,' came the patient reply. 'He had too much of a start on us. Once he got to the courts and back doubles, that was it. Disappeared into the warren.'

'Anything missing?'

'Not that we can tell, sir. Looks like they got in through the roof and out through the back window. Why they made such a noise, I couldn't say.'

Nor could Colonel Radcliffe. All he could do was redouble his efforts to track down the Tolchards.

Jack lay stiff as a scaffold board for a long time after he thought the policeman had gone. So long that he drifted into a shallow sleep. He woke in a panic, knowing that he couldn't hide where he was indefinitely and unsure how much of the night had passed.

Whatever the time was, it was far too late to go to Rupert's house now, so in the end he decided to make his way to the flat roof instead. Perhaps the others would come looking for him there.

He arrived at dawn and, glancing towards the Jevons' yard, felt an ache of nostalgia. Only a few days ago he would have been waking there now, with no fear of the day ahead.

His damaged ankle protested sharply as he climbed the rickety wooden stairs but on reaching the roof he stopped, not in pain but surprise. April and Rupert were already there.

'Where have you been, Jack?' asked April, shocked by his appearance.

Jack slumped down without answering and sat looking up at them for a moment. 'Why are you both here so early?' he asked.

'I've been here all night,' said April.

'And I couldn't sleep,' said Rupert, staring at Jack's gashed arms and bloody ankle. 'What's happened to you?'

Jack shrugged. 'Erskine saw me in the market. I think he had me followed. The same thug who tried to kill my dad. He tried to kill me too.'

April and Rupert glanced at each other, then back at Jack. Then April hurried to the edge of the roof. 'Stay where you are,' she commanded and disappeared. She came back a few minutes later with some damp cotton rags.

'From Mrs Jevons' washing line,' she explained. 'Only borrowed.' And without giving him time to protest, she began to clean and bind Jack's ankle. He was embarrassed by the attention.

'Sit still,' she commanded. 'At least you don't smell of sick this time.'

'Well?' asked Rupert impatiently.

'I went to Nunwell Street,' explained Jack. 'That's where he caught me. But the worst thing is, I couldn't match Erskine's fingerprint. It was too dark to see. So we're no nearer proving him guilty.'

There was an odd silence.

April concentrated on tying knots in rags. Eventually, she looked up at Rupert. 'You tell him,' she said.

'Tell me what?' Jack looked sharply from one to the other.

Rupert cleared his throat. 'April and I went to the shop.'

'Shop?'

'The art shop. Paterson and Jenkins. Where Erskine buys his stuff. He was there at half past ten on Tuesday morning.'

Jack was bewildered. He'd lost track of the days, let alone the hours. He looked at Rupert and at April and shook his head. 'So why's that important?'

'Because it's the time you were in the chimney,' said Rupert flatly. 'It's the time you overheard the conversation. Erskine wasn't there, in his room. He was in the shop.'

Jack took several seconds to come to terms with this. 'But . . . Erskine saw me last night, in the market. I'm sure he did. And then I was followed to Nunwell Street . . . He's *got* to be involved.'

Rupert's reply was steady. 'He wasn't in the room, Jack.'

Arthur Jevons whistled tunelessly as he coaxed the small fire into life and put the kettle on. He always made his own breakfast; he insisted on it. There was enough for his wife to be doing later. Besides, he preferred his own company first thing in the morning.

He heard a knock at the front door and was surprised. He didn't get many callers, especially at dawn. The police again? His wife had told him of their visit yesterday. Jevons had half a mind to ignore whoever it was but there was another knock, louder this time, and he didn't want his family woken. He wheezed to his feet and went to the front door.

Tony Tolchard was on the step. He moved swiftly, furtively, inside without waiting to be invited.

'Is my son here?'

The brisk, accusing tone along with the forced entry immediately angered Jevons.

'No,' he said tersely.

'Where is he then? You're his kind uncle, you should know.'

'I'm not his uncle, kind or otherwise. You're his father. You should know better than anyone.'

Tony merely grunted.

'He's not here,' repeated Jevons firmly as his visitor walked on into the kitchen.

Tony glanced around suspiciously before planting himself on the chair by the fire. 'A cup of tea would be welcome,' he said.

'You've got a nerve,' said Jevons, trying to keep his voice down. 'You take the boy from us, then lose him, then come back here as if it's our fault. And why do the police want him so bad?'

Tony looked up at this. 'Police?'

'Yes, they're after him as well as after you. What kind of trouble have you dragged him into? You're not a father. You're not fit to be a rat in a cellar!'

Tony sprang up and Jevons waited for the punch. It didn't come but he wouldn't have cared if it had.

'Get out of my house,' he gasped, then began to cough uncontrollably.

Instead of leaving, Tony stalked to the back door and out into the yard. Jevons was helpless to stop him.

'If I find him after all . . .' threatened Tony.

Jevons raged against the man and the coughing spasm with equal impotence. Tony had begun to search the sheds, toppling the newspaper stack as he did so.

'Stop it, damn you!' Jevons tried to shout.

From across the lane, Jack heard the noise in Jevons' yard. He even heard Jevons' painful angry cry and thought that for some strange reason he must be shouting at the horse in its stable. But then he heard another voice. Dismissive. Bullying.

'I'll stop when I'm good and ready.'

His father.

'If you've lied to me . . . I'll be back for you.'

Jack heard the yard gate being wrenched open and glimpsed his father's head as he strode away.

April put a quick, cautioning hand on Jack's shoulder but he shrugged it off and scrambled away as swiftly as his bandaged foot and ankle would allow, jumping down on to the next roof.

Tony heard the clattering somewhere behind him and turned in alarm, looking up at the decrepit sheds and shacks that lined the lane. Then something plummeted down and landed in front of him, and his missing son's face was suddenly close to his own.

The face wore an uncharacteristic scowl and the voice was harsh. 'How dare you come here?' it demanded.

Tony managed a smirk. 'I was right then. I knew where to find you. The old wheezer was lying.'

'He doesn't know I'm here,' said Jack. 'Nobody does.' He pulled his startled father out of the lane and pushed him against a wall.

'They're good people. If you've brought the police or worse to their door . . .'

He couldn't finish the threat; he let go of his father.

'Easy, boy, easy,' said Tony soothingly.

He's going to smile, thought Jack. *He's actually going to smile.* He did.

'What's wrong about a father seeking out his son, eh? Eh?' Tony raised his hands to pre-empt the obvious answer. 'All right, all right. Harsh words were said and I walked away from you the other night –'

'You damned me to hell.'

'And I'm here to apologize for that. The worry of it's cost me more than being strangled – or wanted by the crushers – and that's a fact. That's why I had to find you: to put things right between us again.'

The flimsy tin roof above their heads creaked in the morning breeze. Jack wanted to pull it down and bury his father. But he couldn't.

'What do you want?' he asked coldly instead.

'I've told you –'

'What do you *want*?'

Tony regarded him, as if judging what Jack's reaction was likely to be, then his smile became more relaxed. He delved swiftly in his pocket. *He knows I'm going to help*, thought Jack. *Whatever it is, he's sure of me.*

His father produced a small dog-eared card.

'It's what Richard Featherstone gave me, remember? I thought I'd lost it but it was in my jacket lining all the time. I'm owed a fair amount of wages now, Jack. For the days since his father died, plus a week before. I want you to go and get it for me.'

'Go yourself.'

'No, no, look, I can't . . .' He was beginning to wheedle now. The appeal of helplessness.

'There won't be any crushers at Featherstone's place. He's on our side. But it's getting there, that's the thing, Jack. I'm not as quick and clever as you, son. I can't get around like you can, without being spotted.'

'Jack's in just as much danger as you.'

The sharp voice came from behind Tony. He turned to see a well-fed, well-dressed boy and a small, grimy girl. He didn't recognize either of them. It was the girl who had spoken. Her fists were clenched.

'Nice company you're keeping, Jack,' remarked Tony, looking at the girl, unable to help the smirk.

'It's company that cares what happens to him,' said the girl. 'Company what doesn't use him. Your son's been near murdered cos of you, and all you want is for him to do your dirty work while you stay safe.'

'It's the last thing I'll ever ask of you, son,' whined Tony, turning his back on the other two. 'I'll go far away and that's a promise. I won't come near Jevons again. I won't come near you, if that's what you want, though it'll grieve me. But I can't go anywhere without money. So just help me this one last time.'

He held the card towards Jack.

'Don't take it,' said Rupert.

Tony was certain that he would. Jack held his look defiantly, then snatched the card without even glancing at it.

'Where will you go? If I get your wages?'

Tony shrugged easily. 'Why, north, of course, like I told you the other night, when I said we should go together –'

'No!' said Jack.

Tony affected a hurt look at this violent rejection, but he had got what he wanted.

'Bring the money to me by mid-morning.'

'Where?'

Tony shrugged. 'Here's as good a place as any. Bye for now, son.' He patted Jack's shoulder and strolled away.

Jack didn't reply, but the skinny girl quickly followed Tony and as soon as they were out of earshot she grabbed his arm, forcing him to stop.

'Make sure this *is* the last time you bother Jack,'

she said. 'Cos if you don't, you'll end up in a sewer.'

Tony laughed off the threat. But only after the girl had gone.

Jack and Rupert were back on the roof when April joined them. They were looking at the card. It had Richard Featherstone's home address on it: Denmoy House, Portman Square.

'You can't go yet,' reasoned Rupert. 'It's far too early. Try to get a bit of sleep first.'

None of them thought sleep possible but wedged close together for warmth, their tired bodies gave in and they all dozed a little. It was nearly eight o'clock by Rupert's pocket watch when they woke. He hoped his mother wouldn't question the note he'd left, saying he'd gone out early for some exercise.

'Let's go,' said April, scrambling to her feet and stretching her numb limbs. 'Featherstone's bound to be up by now.'

'Not you two.' Jack stood up. 'I'll be quicker on my own.' The stiffness in his ankle suggested otherwise.

'But the police are looking for you,' protested Rupert. 'We can watch for them.'

'No,' said Jack, moving away. 'It would be more useful for you to tackle Erskine.'

Rupert opened his mouth to protest but Jack cut in quickly.

'Yes, I know we have to believe the art shop man. Erskine wasn't in the room so he didn't arrange the murder. But it's still his room. He must know who *was* there while he was out.' He started down the stairs from the flat roof. 'See if you can get him to tell you. I'll meet you back here in a couple of hours.'

And he hurried away, trying not to limp.

Tony Tolchard skulked around for a while, pleased he'd been able to persuade Jack to go for his wages but irritated that he would have to wait. He heard a clock strike eight o'clock. He'd said mid-morning; hours to kill yet, hours to hide from the crushers. He wished he'd said earlier. Then he realized there were things left behind in his old room that could be useful when he went north: his best boots for a start, and his best silk neckerchief. He needed to look presentable in his new life. The more he thought about it, the more necessary a last visit to the room became. He would still be back behind Jevons' yard in plenty of time.

He made his watchful way home. As he drew near, he began to worry that the police might be waiting but there were no uniforms in the street, and none guarding the back alley, which he used in preference to the front door. Only a few workmen yawned and scratched and chatted quietly as they started to mend the road.

Tony sneaked up to his room and found it just as he'd left it. His best boots were still under his bed; the neckerchief in its drawer. Tony put them in his old carpet bag, stuffed in a clean shirt as well, and hurried out.

Jack's birthday clothes were still soaking in their bucket in the backyard. Tony didn't give them a glance as he marched confidently away past the privy – and walked straight into a workman.

'Sorry, sir,' said the man. 'Were you in a hurry?'

The voice disconcerted Tony. He'd heard it before. He peered at the face, partly hidden beneath the narrow-brimmed hat; and recognized Constable Downing.

Rupert dropped Erskine's envelope of receipts on a patch of muddy grass and scuffed it around a little. His story was that he'd found the envelope in his back garden. How it had got there was a mystery. He was merely being a good neighbour and returning it.

Getting to Erskine's front door without his mother seeing him was a difficulty. He approached swiftly from the other end of Calborn Gardens and rapped at the knocker. The housekeeper opened the door, which was a bad start.

'Good morning, Mrs Barnes,' said Rupert brightly. 'Could I possibly see Mr Erskine?'

'What, before breakfast is over?'

'I'd be quite happy to come in and wait.'

'You might be happy, Master Rupert. I wouldn't.'

She closed the door in his face. April, waiting on the opposite side of the road, couldn't suppress a giggle.

'Where were you at seven o'clock last night?' The question was firmly but not aggressively put. Tony Tolchard made out he was thinking, tried to look as if he was being helpful.

'In a pub,' he replied.

'Which pub?'

Tony shrugged. 'Lots. The Grapes, the Drovers, the King George, the Cat and Fiddle –'

'Can anyone confirm any of this?'

Tony smirked. 'You could ask a barmaid or two.'

'We will,' Colonel Radcliffe assured him.

Constables Downing and Adams, standing to attention by the door, listened and watched carefully. Adams glanced at Richard Featherstone. Colonel Radcliffe had sent for him the moment Tolchard was brought in. To ensure fair play for Tolchard, the Colonel had said. But as Richard Featherstone shifted uncomfortably in his chair, looking ill at ease, Adams suddenly wondered if the desire to be seen to be fair was Colonel Radcliffe's only motive.

'You were in a pub three nights ago as well, Mr Tolchard,' said Radcliffe, changing tack sharply, though his voice was as calm as ever. 'The Cap and Cockerel. Before that you were at your place of work. You have been asked this next question more than once; I strongly advise you to think carefully before you answer it again. Did you leave a window open? To be precise, did you leave the back window in the small storeroom on the first floor open?'

'No, sir. Like I told you before. I did not.'

'Are you familiar with the word *forensic*, Mr Tolchard?'

Tony shook his head. 'No, sir.'

'It means scientific evidence acceptable in a court of law.' Colonel Radcliffe paused. 'There is evidence, strong forensic evidence, that the window of the storeroom was locked not from the inside as one would expect, but skilfully from the outside. Which suggests it had been used to facilitate an exit. And, therefore, possibly before that to gain entry. Which in turn suggests it may have been left open beforehand. What about fingerprints, Mr Tolchard?'

Forensic? Fingerprints? Tony felt he was being led on to dangerous unknown ground. He licked his dry lips.

'When we touch something, particularly a smooth surface like, say, a window frame, we leave a mark,' explained Colonel Radcliffe. 'Not always visible to the naked eye, but it's there and it's identifiable, because everyone's mark is different. Now. If I had found many different marks on the window frame in question, I would have to assume that any one of many people could have opened it. But if I had found only *your* fingerprints, Mr Tolchard . . . well, I would have to assume that only *you* could have opened it. Here.' He produced and snapped open a tin. 'Paper please, Adams.'

Constable Adams quickly found a sheet of paper and placed it on the table in front of a very apprehensive Tony.

'Now, Mr Tolchard,' said Radcliffe briskly, 'press your fingers on the pad and then on the paper, if you please. Then I will have a sample of your unique fingerprints.'

Tony slowly, silently shook his head. Radcliffe smiled.

'There's no cause for concern. Only the guilty have anything to fear from fingerprints. But perhaps you would like to see how it's done first? Might I trouble you, Mr Featherstone?'

Richard was startled. 'Me?'

'It would be a great help, sir: for demonstration purposes.'

Richard hesitated then touched the greasy black pad.

'Harder please, sir. We'll clean you up afterwards.'

Richard pressed harder. His hand was shaking slightly. He allowed Radcliffe to remove his hand from the tin and plant his fingers on the paper.

'Constable Downing, some soap and water for Mr Featherstone, please.'

Downing left the room reluctantly. He didn't want to miss Tolchard's turn. It was deeply satisfying to see the smile being wiped off his lying face.

Tony was beginning to sweat. Was this fingerprint thing a trick? He curled his fingers into fists and put them behind his back. He thought he could see now what this foxy policeman was up to. He planned to pin the whole thing on him: Tony Tolchard was going to be done for murder. A murder he hadn't committed.

'Fingerprints please, Mr Tolchard.'

'No,' said Tony. 'You shan't have them.'

Downing stood in the doorway, holding his breath, soap and water forgotten in his hands.

'You don't need them,' blurted Tony. 'I did leave the window open.' His voice rose as he stood up and faced Colonel Radcliffe. 'But I didn't kill the old man. I didn't!' He turned to Richard. 'You've got to believe me, Mr Richard. No one's sorrier for Mr Featherstone's death than me, but I only did what I was asked to do.'

'Asked? Or paid?' Colonel Radcliffe looked calmly at Tony, who sat down again and sniffed.

'All right, money changed hands – but I didn't know what it was for. I swear.'

'The man who paid you to leave the window open,' said Radcliffe. 'What's his name?'

'I don't know his name.' Tony hid his head briefly in his hands. 'But he knows mine. And he knows where I live. Look.' He pulled down his collar to show the vivid bruises on his neck. 'He tried to throttle me. He crept into my lodgings and tried to kill me.' He appealed to Richard for help. 'I only lied because I was scared, Mr Richard, sir. I'm risking my own life in helping you now.'

Richard stared, horrified, at Tony's neck.

'Your selflessness is deeply appreciated,' said Radcliffe with coldest irony. 'Can you give a description?'

'Oh yes,' said Tony. 'I can describe him, don't worry. Right down to his thumbnails.'

When Hugo Erskine stepped outside at nine o'clock, he saw the Shorey boy lurking. There was a small girl with him. Erskine tried to pretend he hadn't seen them, but soon heard their footsteps behind him.

'Excuse me, sir.'

Erskine turned, very displeased, and sighed. 'What on earth do you want now, boy?'

'To return this.' Rupert pulled the grubby envelope of receipts from his pocket and thrust it at Erskine. 'I believe it's yours. I found it in the garden.'

Erskine regarded the envelope for a couple of moments then took it. He was suspicious now as well as annoyed. Rupert forged quickly on. He and April had decided the only way to discover what they wanted to know was to ask a direct question. Even if Erskine didn't answer directly, his reaction might give them some clue.

'And there's something else, sir. Can you tell me who was in your room on Tuesday morning?'

'What?'

'When you were at the art shop?'

Erskine just stared at Rupert.

'Why on earth should I?' he eventually snapped. 'How dare you be so impertinent. Now go away before I call the police.'

'Do that,' said April swiftly, 'and they'll ask you the same question. Cos whoever they were knows about the Nunwell Street murder. And I bet you do too.'

Erskine took an instinctive step back from the fierce, dirty girl.

'*What?* You deserve a beating, you nasty little child. And you too, Master Shorey.'

Rupert stood his ground.

'Who was it, sir?' he asked. 'Please.'

Erskine waved a dismissive hand and walked away.

'Please!' Rupert called after him.

Erskine stopped and turned, his face white with anger.

'Friends,' he said. 'And one of them was Richard Featherstone. Are you suggesting he killed his own father?'

'Explain to me again about last night,' said Colonel Radcliffe.

Tony's decision to tell the truth about the window didn't seem to have satisfied the man at all.

'I've told you,' he sighed. 'I got drunk and fell asleep.'

'Your son was at seventeen Nunwell Street. Can you explain why?'

'My son? Jack?' The interview was taking too many twists and turns for Tony.

'He was identified leaving the premises. He and another person broke in and disturbed the scene of crime. You're very close, I understand. You and Jack. Father and son. You do things together.'

Tony began to panic. 'Yes. I mean no . . . No. I wasn't anywhere near Nunwell Street last night. I swear.'

'Then who else can have been with the boy?'

Colonel Radcliffe was wandering around the room now. 'You're quite sure, Mr Tolchard, you weren't visiting the scene of the murder? Or maybe revisiting it. With the help of an agile and dutiful son?'

'No!' Tony's voice was almost a squeak.

'Of course,' said Radcliffe carefully, 'we could ask Jack ourselves. If only we knew where he was.' He stared softly, hopefully, at Tony. And waited.

'Redbarn Road.' Tony lowered his eyes. 'You'll find him at Redbarn Road. Up on the old buildings behind the sweep's yard – Jevons' place. He'll be waiting there with my wages.' He glanced humbly at Richard. 'I sent him to your house, Mr Richard. I hope the money'll be paid in your absence as you said before?'

Richard merely nodded. There was a brief silence, then Colonel Radcliffe turned to him.

'So it seems we must go to Redbarn Road, Mr Featherstone. Will you accompany us to ensure we're as fair with the son as you'll no doubt agree we've been with the father?'

Richard was looking pale and unwell. He shook his head. 'That won't be necessary, Colonel. You've more than proved yourself as even-handed.'

He managed to stand up. 'You'll understand these . . . revelations come as something of a shock. If you'll excuse me.'

He picked up his hat and left. Radcliffe watched him go, then spoke quietly to Adams before turning briskly to Downing.

'Handcuffs for Mr Tolchard, please, Downing. He's coming with us to Redbarn Road.'

Tony was appalled. 'You can't take me with you,' he cried. 'Jack'll think I've betrayed him.'

'You have,' said Radcliffe tersely. 'Probably all his life.'

Portman Square was full of fine buildings and Denmoy House, the Featherstones' residence, was just about the finest.

Jack stood a moment, gazing up at it. The tradesmen's entrance was down a flight of steps between railings. Jack went down the steps, pulled the bell handle and waited. Some time after the distant jangle had faded inside the house, the door was opened by a man with neat hair and a long black apron. He had silver polish on his fingers. Jack judged him to be the butler.

'Excuse me, sir. My name's Jack Tolchard. Tony Tolchard's son?'

The man's face remained suspicious but Jack was relieved to see a glimmer of recognition at the name.

He held out the card.

'Mr Richard gave my father this and said he was to come for his wages.'

The butler took the card delicately between finger and thumb. 'So where is your father?'

'He's unwell, sir.'

The butler handed back the card. 'Mr Richard is out at the moment but he has left instructions. Step inside.' He closed and locked the door with Jack inside the house.

'Wait here,' he said, and turned unhurriedly away.

Jack watched the butler disappear towards a passage, then heard his footsteps mounting stairs. He'd been left alone in a large scullery. To his right a doorway opened into a huge circular room flooded with morning light, which streamed through its high glass ceiling. From where he stood, Jack could see that the walls were lined with paintings. Curious, he walked across and went in, then stopped and stared in utter surprise.

The same workmen and street entertainers who had gazed at him from the paintings in Erskine's room were gazing down at him from these walls too: singers were singing and scaffolders were eating their lunch. His eyes lingered on a picture of a man swallowing a snake. That one was different. He shuddered and moved his gaze on.

Then the whole world seemed to close in on him. He was staring at a picture of a strongman lying on a small stage with a paving slab on his chest. The man's hands gripped the edge of the slab, braced to take the blow from the hammer that was about to smash down on it. It was the hands Jack recognized first. He began to feel cold, as if ice were sliding down his back. There was no mistaking those huge hands or the straining face turned sideways, looking out of the canvas at him. He was staring again directly into the eyes of the man who had followed him to Nunwell Street. The man who'd tried to kill his father.

Collision

Jack had moved involuntarily away from the painting, as if the man could reach out from the wall and grab him. He moved closer again.

'Were you told you could come in here?'

Jack jumped and spun round, ready to run. Richard Featherstone was standing in the doorway.

'I'm sorry, sir. I'm only looking at the paintings.'

Richard approached across the room, his heels tapping loudly on the tiled floor.

'And do you like what you see?'

'Yes, sir.'

'Especially that one?'

'Um . . . yes, sir. Do you know the man, sir?'

'A strange question from a trespasser.'

Richard was behind him now.

'Mr Richard?' The butler's surprised voice startled them both. He was standing in the doorway, a stout paper bag full of coins in his hand. 'I didn't hear you come in, sir.' He stepped forward anxiously. 'You look unwell. May I fetch you something?'

'No. I'm quite well, thank you, Parfitt,' said Richard, attempting a smile. 'And I would like to speak to this young man alone.'

'Are you quite sure, sir?'

'I am.' Richard took the bag of money, then shut the door behind the departing butler. He came and stood beside Jack.

'I've just returned from the police station, Jack – may I call you Jack?'

Jack nodded warily.

'I'm told that you broke into my father's office last night. Why did you do that?'

Jack felt his cheeks go red but he said nothing.

'Did you hope to find money – or valuables? Or were you merely curious to see the site of such a terrible crime?'

Jack stared at the floor.

'Your father is with the police now.'

Jack looked up slowly. Was this a trick?

'He swears he wasn't the man they saw with you last night,' said Richard. 'The police don't believe him, of course.'

Jack's face betrayed his anxiety but still he said nothing.

'If you're trying to protect him, you're wasting your silence. He's confessed to leaving a window open. Someone paid him to.'

174

Jack took a deep breath and looked straight at Richard. 'I'm sorry he did that, sir. He's not a bad man. I truly believe he didn't know what a terrible thing was going to happen.'

Richard regarded the boy in front of him with an almost detached curiosity. The father was obviously so indifferent to his son's fate and yet the son was so loyal. He shook his head and began to laugh. How different their circumstances were. His own father had been a good man and in his own way a good father too. And yet how disloyal the son.

Jack stepped back, unnerved by the sudden strange laughter. He saw tears on the man's cheeks. Richard choked them back. Then the laughter stopped too.

'Why do you want to know about Mr Davis?' he asked.

Jack was totally thrown by the question. 'Mr Davis?'

Richard nodded at the painting. 'The man beneath the paving slab.'

Jack hesitated. 'Because, sir, I'm afraid he may have had something to do with your father's death.'

Richard said nothing. Jack blundered on.

'And, sir, it's possible that Mr Erskine, the artist, was also involved.'

The bag of money hit the floor with a thud

and split open. Coins, silver and copper, rolled noisily across the hard tiles. Richard's face, already pale, had turned grey. He stared at Jack until the last coin had fallen still. After a brief silence, he gestured at the walls and whispered: 'These are not Erskine's work, Jack. He's a good artist and a good friend but he didn't paint these. I did. They are all *my* paintings. I painted John Davis; his hands, his cruel eyes, his strength . . .' He paused. 'Are you saying *I* killed my father?'

Suddenly, the new and awful possibility became clear to Jack. It could have been Richard Featherstone he'd heard from inside the chimney. Richard Featherstone, Erskine's friend, and Davis the man they both painted.

'Are you?' Richard was waiting for an answer.

'No, sir.' Jack hesitated, staring back at the trembling man. 'I believe someone paid John Davis to kill him.'

Richard began to laugh again. 'Like someone paid *your* father to leave the window open?'

'John Davis paid my father to leave the window open.'

The laughter stopped abruptly.

'You can't know that.'

'I do, sir.'

Richard turned away. He paced in silence for a few moments.

'Tell me, Jack. If John Davis paid your father

to leave the window open, who do you think paid John Davis to murder my father?'

Jack feared to say, although he felt sure now. He wished the door was closer. Richard suddenly caught hold of his arm.

'You can be frank with me, Jack.' The strange, almost hysterical tears were flowing again. 'We share an interest in troublesome fathers, I think.'

He let go of Jack's arm, sniffed and wiped his face with his hand. 'It can be a terrible thing to be a son, don't you agree? Fathers so seldom behave as one would wish. As one would behave oneself. Indeed, sometimes it seems they set out deliberately to thwart, frustrate and generally belittle, when they have it in their hands to do so much more ... D'you not feel that fathers are not fit to hold such power over us?'

Richard paused then laughed again. 'I read your thoughts, Jack. Where's the comparison, you're thinking. But the thing is, Jack, mine was every bit as selfish as your own appears to be. Mine pursued his own desires to the exclusion of all else. And his latest desire was to hazard everything on two strips of steel to run the length of South America. His entire fortune – and this house as well – were to be gambled for no better reason than the thrill he got from risk. All or nothing. Never mind his family, never mind art and beauty.'

He swept his hand around the room. 'He

knew, he *knew* how many artists depended on our money. Not just my friends, dozens of others as well who would be destitute without my patronage. I have no income of my own. I relied on his great wealth. But those I support were of no account to him. *I* was of no account.' He turned his head aside. 'I didn't plan to do it, don't think that of me. I'm not cold-blooded.' He choked back a sob, then grabbed Jack's wrist and pulled him close.

'Understand this, Jack. Hugo Erskine knows nothing. I was at the house where he's working. John Davis was there too. We both paint Davis frequently. We were discussing my latest project. Hugo went out to pick up some materials he'd ordered. I went on chatting to Davis . . . And then it came to me. He's so strong, so fearless. So ruthless. It suddenly seemed the obvious solution. I didn't stop to think about it. I made a wild decision. And how I wish I hadn't . . .'

The room was filled with a thick heavy silence. Then someone began to clap, not loudly, but lightly and slowly.

'Very touching.'

John Davis was standing in the open doorway. His clothes were torn and filthy and his clapping hands were bloody. Richard stared at him, unable to speak.

'My blood this time, Mr Featherstone,' Davis

whispered, coming into the room and closing the door behind him. He held his hands up for Richard to see better. 'You'll excuse my coming in without disturbing the staff.'

Jack's heart began to pound. He glanced quickly around the room.

'No good looking for another door, boy,' growled Davis. 'There's only one. And no window this time.'

Jack said nothing but tensed his body for the attack he was sure would be launched at any moment.

'This time?' echoed Richard, his voice tight. 'You've met before?'

Davis smiled a hard little smile. 'Tell it your way if you like, boy.'

'Two nights ago I came home,' said Jack, keeping his voice as level as he could, 'and found this man trying to strangle my father.'

Richard gazed at Davis in bewilderment.

'Frighten him,' he whispered. 'He was talking too much in the public house. I told you to follow and *frighten* him, that's all. To keep him silent.'

Davis smirked. 'I frightened him all right.'

'Then last night,' continued Jack, 'he tried to kill me too.'

'Careless, weren't you?' Davis sneered. 'Coming to the market. Not so clever as you think you are, chimney creeper.'

'Why?' demanded Richard. 'Why would you want to harm the boy?'

Davis looked at him pityingly. 'He saw my face, didn't he? He could describe me to the crushers, tell 'em who had paid his miserable dad to leave the window open.' He snorted. 'And they're not stupid any more. If they got me, they'd never let it go. Not till I'd told them the rest. Like who I was working for. Which I would. I don't believe in hanging without company.'

Richard had stopped listening. He couldn't take his eyes off Davis's bloody hands but it wasn't those hands he was seeing. It was his father's battered body. He closed his eyes but that was worse. He could see his father's face smiling out of a pool of redness. Smiling.

'Why did you have to hit my father so hard?' he cried suddenly.

'Because he put up a fight, of course. He had pluck, your father.'

'But so much blood!'

'Oh, I beg your pardon,' said Davis sarcastically. 'Did you think I could kill him and lay him out all pretty, with flowers in his hands and not a mark on his face?'

'I told you,' said Richard. 'It was for the artists who depend on me. For art itself –'

Davis spat on the floor. 'You paid for a murder, not for a painting.'

Jack stared at the shiny gob of saliva but dared not move.

Richard said nothing. He looked up at the glass roof that arched over his studio and as he stared he lost focus and it began to look like a different roof altogether. A station roof. He could see his father again, standing on a railway line that stretched into the distance. The railways had been Henry Featherstone's greatest passion and not just because they made him money. The soaring glass roofs of King's Cross and the rest contained an echoing bustle of life, a richness of movement and purpose, the very things that Richard tried, and usually failed, to celebrate in paint. The railways, with their cheap, fast travel, benefited the working man so close to Richard's heart as much as they benefited the wealthy. They opened up the world. Suddenly Richard realized his father had known that all along. His father's had been the true understanding of what ordinary people needed most. And what had he, the son, achieved on their behalf? Nothing. He'd merely patronized them with his paintings.

Richard could vaguely hear Davis shouting, then the man's great bloodied fists had grabbed his arms and were shaking him.

'Pull yourself together!' roared Davis in his face, 'Or we're both dead!'

'What do you want from me?' moaned Richard.

'A hiding place,' demanded Davis. 'Or distance between me and London. And money to make that possible.'

Richard shook his head. 'I've already paid you. I have no more money in the house. Only what's on the floor.'

Davis kicked out contemptuously at the scattered silver and copper coins.

'Your bank then.' Ripping the scarf from his neck, he twisted Richard round and roughly tied his wrists together behind his back, then began shoving him towards the door. 'We'll go to your bank for some proper cash, and then away. Where's your carriage?'

Jack sprang after them but Davis kicked out viciously and sent him sprawling. He staggered to his feet and tried to follow. As the studio door opened, it seemed to Jack that a dozen people were converging on the scullery, alerted by the shouting, but no one was brave enough to attempt to stop Davis as he bundled Richard out towards the stable yard behind the house. The horses were still harnessed to the smart green carriage and the coachman was standing beside the door, awaiting further orders. Davis pushed Richard roughly inside, punched the protesting coachman, hoisted himself up on to the box seat and grabbed the reins. He slapped them hard and roared and the startled horses leapt forward, careering the carriage behind them out into the street.

Jack hurtled after it. He ran alongside, leapt on to the boarding step, and dived head first through the open window. Davis, intent on driving the horses ever faster, didn't see him.

Richard was lying face down on the floor. Jack swiftly untied the scarf round his wrists and helped him on to the seat.

'You've got to get out,' he panted. 'Davis will kill you for certain.'

Richard stared, uncomprehending. Why did this boy, who knew of his terrible sin, care whether he lived or died?

'The traffic will slow him,' said Jack. 'Be ready to jump.'

But Davis didn't let the traffic slow him. He kept whipping the horses till they were wide-eyed and lunging.

He'd changed his mind about the bank. It was too risky. He veered off the main road and into familiar backstreets heading for King's Cross station. He had enough of a start to be on a train and away before anyone could stop him. Redbarn Road was a good short cut.

'We should have gone to the police!'

April hardly had breath to say what she and Rupert were both thinking as they ran. They'd agonized after Erskine's revelation that Richard Featherstone had been in the room. Should they return to the flat roof as arranged, or tell the police that Jack had unwittingly gone to the house of a man who'd commissioned murder? But it was too late now, they were almost at Jevons' yard. Perhaps Jack had returned safely, after all.

They slowed as they saw the sweep's cart emerge slowly from the lane into Redbarn Road. Jevons didn't see the green carriage hurtling towards him. Nor did his horse. Nor did Rupert or April. One moment the narrow street was empty, the next the carriage seemed to fill it, bearing down on them headlong. There was no way it could stop. The driver didn't even try.

'Go on, damn you!' he screamed, lashing his terrified horses, but at the last moment they panicked, their sweating bodies rearing away to avoid the collision. The carriage slewed sideways, its wheels skidding and cracking, then slammed into the sweep's cart and overturned, while the sweep's cart itself ended crushed against the nearest wall.

Davis leapt from the carriage as it toppled, landing deftly on his feet near Rupert and April. For a moment there was a terrible silence, broken only by Jevons' wheezing as he tried to extricate himself and free his frightened horse. Then another carriage came rapidly into view and half a dozen men, dressed as labourers, jumped down before it stopped. Davis didn't need to look twice: labourers didn't travel by carriage. Somehow, the crushers were here in force.

He saw a face he recognized at the carriage window. Tony Tolchard. And he saw Tolchard's lips move. Then a lean and smart older man leapt from the carriage and pointed towards Davis.

'Take him!'

Davis turned to run, then saw an opportunity and seized it.

April realized too late the danger she was in. Davis had grabbed her arm.

'Not a step closer,' he yelled at the approaching police.

He backed away, dragging April with him. Rupert bravely made to move after them.

'Not one step!' Davis warned again, and Rupert stopped.

April wriggled and kicked and Davis jerked her arm harder.

'Cut that,' he snarled, retreating into the maze of alleys and crumbling, boarded-up buildings across the lane from Jevons' yard. He was familiar with Redbarn Road, but not with this wedge of abandoned property behind it, and suddenly feared he was blundering into a dead end. He had to get up higher, to see the lie of the land, find an escape route. He crashed through a rotten fence, then climbed a wooden staircase, little more than a ladder. The treads were rotten and April screamed as her foot went through.

'Cut the noise as well,' warned Davis as he pulled her roughly upwards.

Constable Adams was closest behind the fugitive and hostage. He heard April's cry and glimpsed her as Davis yanked her away towards the rooftops. Colonel Radcliffe joined him.

'Shall I follow, sir?' asked Adams.

Radcliffe shook his head. 'Not yet. We can't risk the girl.'

As Davis climbed higher, a new dread filled April: her fear of heights. She ceased trying to break free from her captor's grip and clung, shaking and whimpering, to the nearest broken wall. Davis gave her arm a violent shake.

'Move, damn you!'

But April couldn't move. Her legs were trembling and the distant ground seemed to pull her towards it.

'Don't look down.'

Straining upwards, Davis didn't hear the whisper, but April did. Jack was close by, crouched behind a crumbling chimney stack.

'He'll shove you off if you don't go with him,' mouthed Jack. 'Look up, not down. You can do it.'

Davis turned sharply but saw only the trembling girl. Jack had disappeared. Davis gripped April's arm even tighter and tugged viciously. April stared up at the sky and allowed herself to be dragged higher.

Behind them, Jack found a different route, risking a swift clamber up a gable of broken slates until he was clinging beneath the ridge from where he could look down on Davis and April. He saw them emerge on to an area of flat roof at the end of the block, and heard Davis curse loudly as he realized he had trapped himself on high as surely as in a cul-de-sac at ground level. Between him and the next block was a wide gap. Below the gap, a drop that no one could survive. With or without the girl, he would have to leap the gap to escape. He hesitated. He didn't know if he could do it.

Davis looked down at the street beneath him, at the expectant police, the well-dressed boy kneeling beside the wretched sweep, at Richard Featherstone standing unscathed beside the carriage. Tony Tolchard was there too. Davis spat into space and gauged the gap again. He would beat the lot of them yet.

'The boy's up there too,' murmured Richard, gazing upwards in awe. 'Davis hasn't seen him.' Constable Downing, standing close by, nodded.

'Aye,' he said quietly, with a glance at Tony

beside him. 'Glory knows where he gets his courage from.'

He'd removed the handcuffs while in the carriage, so that Jack would suspect nothing when his father appeared. Circumstances had suddenly changed but no one had ordered him to reapply the cuffs. Not even Tolchard would think of escape while his son was risking his life.

High above, Davis loosened his grip on April's arm.

'We're going to jump,' he told her roughly. 'You first.'

April looked down and recoiled. She stumbled backwards from the edge, breaking free of Davis, and Jack saw his chance. He balanced on his toes, then launched himself from the gable end and crashed down on the strongman, knocking him off his feet.

A gasp of admiration and fear ran through the watchers below.

Davis quickly recovered and tried to get his hands round Jack's neck. Locked together, they rolled away from the edge of the roof, then back towards it.

Constable Adams, panting hard, appeared on the roof beside April. Davis saw him, tore himself away from Jack's grip and leapt at the gap. He landed heavily on the other side, his boots dislodging bricks and mortar. The loose stone blocks gave way beneath him and his feet followed. Mortar and masonry showered down into the alleyway below.

Davis cried out and grabbed desperately for some kind of handhold. As he did so, he was aware of someone hurtling over him. Jack landed lightly on all fours, well away from the crumbling edge and, turning to Davis, grabbed him by the scruff of the neck, trying to drag him to safety. But the more Davis struggled to get a foothold, the more of the fragile brickwork beneath him he kicked away and suddenly, amid shouts of alarm from below, a small avalanche of bricks and blocks and rotten window frames cascaded away from under his boots. The small flat roof itself caved in and Davis and Jack tumbled downwards amid the rubble. Nothing fell on top of them and Davis was briefly elated to find himself back on the ground. He turned and grabbed Jack, still coughing in a cloud of brick dust. One hostage was as good as another. Davis dived in through the gaping side of the building, dodging the great wooden props that shored the remainder of it up, and pulled Jack behind him out into Redbarn Road.

Richard Featherstone was the first to see him.

Davis stepped back against the wall, recovering breath. He would demand safe passage in return for the boy's life. But before he could speak, he saw Richard shouting, then running towards him. Davis was momentarily confused. He heard a heavy creaking noise above him, felt the wooden prop beside him shift. Then Featherstone was on him, a Featherstone he didn't recognize, tearing Jack from him and hurling the boy out into the road.

'Get away, Jack! Get away!'

Richard's screaming voice was drowned in the roar from above. He clung to Davis with all the strength he'd never used in his life before, pressing him back against the moving wall; away from Jack; away from escape.

As Jack stumbled clear and turned, he saw the whole frontage of the shored-up building slowly collapse. Then the two men straining against it disappeared beneath a hundred tons of falling, roaring brickwork.

'Here, get this down, boy.'

The words banged into Jack's brain. They were the very words his father had used in the Cap and Cockerel as he forced the first pint of beer into his hand. But this wasn't his father's voice. His father had sneaked away, not knowing if his son were dead or alive. Through the swirling dust and falling masonry, Jack had glimpsed him running off down the street when everyone was looking the other way.

Jack didn't know what he felt about this latest desertion; but it was Arthur Jevons standing in front of him now, a large mug of tea in his hand.

'There's plenty of milk and sugar in it,' he said kindly. 'Best thing for shock.'

'Go on, Jack. Drink it.' Rupert was sitting on a small stool beside him.

April was sitting on an even smaller stool on his other side, eating a thick slice of bread and jam.

'It'll do you good,' she said.

Jack silently took the mug and glanced around. The Jevons' house had never been so crowded. The yard gate was propped open and policemen bustled in and out past Mrs Jevons and her small children. Jack didn't remember getting from Redbarn Road to his old home. He didn't remember much after Richard Featherstone's scream and the glimpse of his fleeing father.

'Where's Davis?' he asked suddenly.

Rupert was relieved to hear him speak at last.

'He's dead,' he replied. 'Under the wall. Richard Featherstone too. The police are still digging but there's no hope.'

Jack nodded. Then he said: 'You know it was them I overheard?'

'Yes,' said April. 'We've told the Colonel man about that, and everything else we know too.'

Jack stared at her in surprise.

'When?'

'Since we've been here in Mr Jevons' house,' she replied, licking jam from her fingers. 'You've missed the last half hour. Shock, like Mr Jevons said.'

'Colonel Radcliffe, that's him over there in the smart clothes,' said Rupert quietly. 'He asked Mr Jevons if everyone could come in here while we wait for transport to the police station.'

'Oh.'

'We've said about the grapnel too,' added April. 'I'm going to show a crusher where it is a bit later.'

'It's almost bound to have Davis's fingerprints on it,' added Rupert, 'which will prove he used it to get to the window.'

'Oh.'

Jack was finding it all a bit much to take in. He sat in silence for a moment then turned to April. 'How did you get down?'

April nodded at Constable Adams, who was standing nearby. 'He gave me a hand.' Then she blushed and admitted crossly: 'No, he didn't give me a hand. He carried me down like a baby.'

Jack smiled and shared a look with Rupert.

'You are allowed to have things you can't do,' he suggested.

April wrinkled her nose. 'No. Never.'

Colonel Radcliffe heard their voices and came over to them.

'Ah . . . Master Jack Tolchard . . . No, don't get up.' He crouched down in front of Jack.

'You know we were looking for you?' he said seriously. 'That a warrant was out for your arrest?'

'Sir.' Jack sat very still.

'Breaking and entering is a serious crime,' continued Colonel Radcliffe quietly, 'which carries severe penalties.' He looked hard at Jack. 'There was a disturbance in Nunwell Street last night and one of my officers thought he saw you in the vicinity.'

Jack licked his lips but said nothing. Constable Adams was now standing next to the Assistant Commissioner. Radcliffe looked up at him.

'Are you able to identify Jack Tolchard as the boy you saw?' he asked. 'Able to identify him positively. Absolutely positively. Without any shadow of doubt?'

Adams stared down at the Colonel and hoped he was reading the clues correctly.

'No, sir,' he said, standing to attention. 'Not absolutely and finally positively.'

Colonel Radcliffe nodded.

'In that case, we shan't need to mention the matter again.' He smiled and stood up. 'Do you have any questions, Jack?'

Jack shook his head, then as the Assistant Commissioner turned away, he suddenly said:

'Sir. There won't be trouble for Mr Jevons, will there? He's a good master and never, ever, asked me to climb a chimney.'

The Colonel smiled again and shook his head.

'Thank you.' Jack hesitated. 'And there's my father. What will happen to him?'

Colonel Radcliffe shrugged, briefly grim. 'He's done himself no good by running off,' he said. 'But before that, he helped us, so I'll do my very best to ensure he doesn't hang for his part in it all.' He patted Jack on the shoulder, then put out his hand for Jack to shake. 'And for your own part, lad, well done.'

April snorted as Radcliffe walked away. 'They've got to catch him first.' She shrugged. 'Still, so long as he doesn't come near you again I don't care what happens to him.'

They sat in silence for a moment then Rupert spoke.

'What about you, Jack?' His voice betrayed his concern. 'You haven't even got a room to go back to now. Where will you live?'

'There's room here for him if he wants,' wheezed Jevons, standing over them. He was holding a mug of tea and a thick jam sandwich which he thrust at Rupert. 'Here, I expect you need a bit of sustenance too.' He took a deep, noisy breath. 'Goodness knows how we'll make a living without a cart, though. All I've got left is Old Duke and a pile of matchwood. But Jack's more than welcome.'

Jack got unsteadily to his feet. He wanted to say there was nothing in the world he would like better, but before he could speak, a loud male voice boomed from the lane.

'Is this the place?'

'Oh, gosh. It's my pa.' Rupert stood up, mug in one hand, jam sandwich in the other, and waited for the inevitable.

It took some time to explain to Mr Shorey why his son was not at school but drinking tea in a sweep's kitchen. Rupert let the Assistant Commissioner do all the talking.

'Nasty business,' said Mr Shorey. He turned to his wife. 'I told you we should have sent him to boarding school. You don't get mixed up in things like this at boarding school.'

'No, dear,' murmured Mrs Shorey.

'Ma?' Rupert spoke suddenly to his mother. 'You agree, don't you, that Mr Jevons is the best sweep you've ever had?'

'Yes, dear.' Mrs Shorey nodded vaguely. She hadn't given the matter much thought but her son looked rather serious.

'Well, without his cart, he can't work and we

can't have our chimneys swept properly. Can we buy him a cart?'

'What?' Mr Shorey glared at his son.

'You can take it from my pocket money, Pa,' said Rupert. 'For as long as necessary.'

Mrs Shorey looked around the little home and at the jam sandwich in her son's hand; generosity from people with so little to give.

'I'm sure we can help purchase a cart,' she said. 'Possibly one of those new sweeping machines too.' She turned brightly to her husband. 'After all, dear, think how much we save by not sending Rupe to boarding school.'

Mr Shorey stared open-mouthed at his wife. Then a small voice broke the silence.

'Rupe!' April was trying not to giggle. 'You never said you get called *Rupe*.'

Rupert pretended not to hear. 'And what are *you* going to do, April?' he asked. 'Apart from look after your gran.'

April thought for a moment.

'I shall solve another crime,' she said. 'One with a proper reward next time.' She paused. 'You can help if you like, Rupe.' She turned to the sweep's boy and nodded. 'And so can Scarper Jack.'

Only the strong will survive...

Born a boy. Raised with dogs. Became a hero.

BRIND and the DOGS of WAR

CHRISTOPHER RUSSELL

The second adventure of Brind the dog boy

YEAR OF THE BLACK DEATH — THE WORST TIME TO BE ALIVE

PLAGUE SORCERER

CHRISTOPHER RUSSELL

'It's dangerous,' said Reuben quietly.
'Transportation to the colonies
if we're caught. Or hanging.'

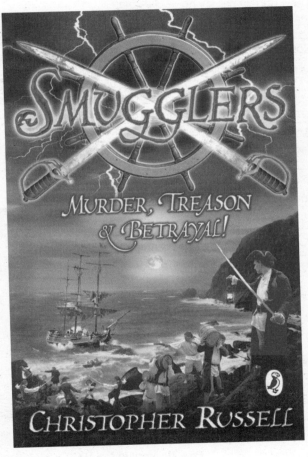

Shortlisted for the
Waterstone's Children's Book Prize

puffin.co.uk

Puffin by Post

Scarper Jack and the Bloodstained Room – Christopher Russell

If you have enjoyed this book and want to read more,
then check out these other great Puffin titles.
You can order any of the following books direct with Puffin by Post:

Brind and the Dogs of War • Christopher Russell • 9780141318547	£5.99
'Original and hugely satisfying' – *Guardian*	

Plague Sorcerer • Christopher Russell • 9780141318554	£4.99
'Admirably vivid – cliff-hanging action' – *Books for Keeps*	

Smugglers • Christopher Russell • 9780141320953	£4.99
Murder, treason and betrayal! Shortlisted for the Waterstone's Children's Book Prize	

The Devil's Breath • David Gilman • 9780141323022	£6.99
'Heart-pounding action' – *The Times*	

Half Moon Investigations • Eoin Colfer • 9780141320809	£5.99
'Wickedly brilliant' – *Independent*	

Just contact:

Puffin Books, C/o Bookpost, PO Box 29,
Douglas, Isle of Man, IM99 1BQ
Credit cards accepted. For further details:
Telephone: 01624 677237
Fax: 01624 670923

You can email your orders to: bookshop@enterprise.net
Or order online at: www.bookpost.co.uk

Free delivery in the UK.
Overseas customers must add £2 per book.

Prices and availability are subject to change.

Visit puffin.co.uk to find out about the latest titles, read extracts and
exclusive author interviews, and enter exciting competitions.
You can also browse thousands of Puffin books online.